Origin Journey

Origin

Journey

Scot Simpson

ISBN: 978-0-578-30861-6

Printed in the United States of America

Acknowledgments

The first to travel with the Zeposze was the "Fam": Leah, Nicole, Matt, Shea, Lara, and Kiera. They gave me my first redirection and encouragement. Catherine Kean, my developmental editor, came next and instigated some major changes. Her friend, Sue-Ellen Welfonder, did the copy edit and was my biggest fan. Lynnette Horner polished it off with a proofread.

Adam Miklasz and I went back and forth many times coming up with the cover art, but I liked his work so much I included it for the chapter covers.

I felt lucky to have all the advice that I received.

Thanks, all of you.

Contents
Origin Journey

Foreword

I spent my entire life writing this book but did not finish page one until I retired. It is a sci-fi romance with a lively young group of Arzolans on an interstellar journey that takes them on many exciting and adventurous excursions. Intermingled with the exhilaration and romance is a subtle presentation of an origin theory of the Universe, of our species, of the megaliths on Earth and an original look at evolution to mutual life. It is an enjoyable adventure that will start you thinking about parts of your own existence.

Scot

PS: *The first letter of each Arzolan name is the same as their hereditary order.*
*The second letter is **r** for male or **s** for female.*

 # - indicates communication by cerebral waves outside of the Cowav.

*Please reference the **Index** in the back for Arzolan norms and translations.*

CHAPTER 1
ARZOLA

Chapter 1 Arzola

Sisual Slammers

City of Kufina
National Sisual Orb

The whole orb shook with the slam.

Mrik winced with the thousands of fans as Arlam recovered. He leaped for the ball right in front of them, catching it with both hands and grabbing a pole in the middle of the orb with his feet. Not about to let a little slam slow him down, he threw the ball to a teammate closer to the goal just before getting slammed again.

Opposing voices grew and ricocheted off the inside of the National Sisual Orb. The Orb was immense, although small compared to the pyramid-shaped Empyramis, the journey ship, that sat nearby.

Trelo, as a Tradan, got good seats for all of the Zeposze, hanging from the top of the orb. They were just three rows down and close to the goal. They looked through the transparent shield into the midst of the action. This was the first time in many years that their Ciles team had made it to the final tournament.

Arlam was at the end of his career. Mrik saw concern in his expression but felt the excitement radiating from his body. He knew he had to win the game today to go on to the championship game next week, but either way, his Sisual activities would end. He and the rest of the Zeposze, the name they called themselves, would be off on a ten-year journey. All eight of them were looking forward to their time aboard the Empyramis, knowing that after the expedition they would be ending their single years and starting their fifty years of united life. For Mrik it would be a ten-year diversion from uniting and the responsibilities a family creates.

The crowd cheered. Arlam jumped just in time to catch the ball with his feet. He grabbed a central pole and readied to fling himself upward. His opponent was finishing a large swing and was just able to reach the ball with his foot and knock it from Arlam's hands. The ball bounced down. One of Arlam's teammates grabbed it but was in trouble as an approaching opponent swung and headed directly for the ball.

Arlam positioned himself, reached out to catch a pass, and quickly shot.

"Score!" Mrik yelled, lunging to his feet.

The Ciles fans were few compared with the Kufina fans, but with that score, their cheers bounced off the top of the Orb. While Kufina was the home team, the Ciles fans carried the excitement.

Arlam hung, swung, threw, and slammed so quickly it was hard to keep up with him—especially with the many diversions like that elegant Politan over there with the most elaborate topper. It was beyond the elegance of the normal Politan topper and created an aura above and around her stunning face.

Mrik thought he caught her eye. Did she sense that he was from Ciles? Maybe she was curious about a Militan from a small town on the other side of the planet. The ladies here in the capital were in a different reality. Not a reality he was familiar with, but one that intrigued him. She was striking. He sure would like to connect with her.

Arlam got slammed again into the invisible barrier between the field and the spectators. Ssflora cringed. Arlam recovered and passed the ball to his teammate, who shot but missed.

Of all the Zeposze, Mrik liked sitting next to Ssflora and Bruid the most. Ssflora always presented a striking image with her delicate sunfus wrapped around her slender body and her smooth but elegant facial lines. Bruid had the most analytic wisdom of all of them, and his comments were enlightening.

Arlam's intensity had risen with that last slam. His speed and agility energized him against the heavier opponents who seemed to tire, as one missed him and slammed into the barrier.

The opponents had a three-goals-to-two advantage, but the Ciles team was starting to fare better. Arlam always said the real game is played after you spend some time learning the opposing players. Our team was invigorated by that last slam and caught up.

The score was four to four. Down to the last point.

The crowd's cheering grew louder. Mrik saw what was developing: Arlam's signature move. A very risky move, but there he was on the far side as his opponent worked his way up the middle. Arlam's teammates were faking the ability to stop the rival's drive.

Arlam started his swing. Timing was crucial. He swung around one pole then another, gaining maximum momentum. On the last swing, he slammed into his opponent just as he was ready to score. Arlam grabbed the ball and scored.

We went wild. Arlam always thought that he would win, but his beaming smile showed a special triumph.

Now Arlam must start thinking about his final game next week. No one wanted to distract him from those thoughts but they were able to get him away for a celebration with the Zeposze. They gathered at a small Relux and celebrated with their favorite hlyusir drink. While swaying with the music, they discussed their future ten-year adventure and remembered their childhood together, when they explored life on Arzola.

"What are you going to do on our journey without sisual to play?" Sslora asked.

Arlam smiled. "I'm going to rely on you and the rest of the Zeposze to keep me entertained."

"Hrlur is the entertainer," Mrik said. "What is your plan for entertainment, Hrlur?"

"Just because I provide eloquent creative art that you laugh at does not mean that I am going to be your jokester," Hrlur said.

"I think you are right, Hrlur," Tsizmelia said. "We should put Mrik in charge of laughter. He is definitely the Zeposze most in need of merriment."

"'Funny' is definitely not part of my military arsenal. I struggle to laugh even at humorous statements, but Tsizmelia, when you are trading, a joke now and then could certainly lubricate the exchange."

"I enjoy when I am able to summon an appropriate joke," Tsizmelia said, "but seeing you struggle with humor is more entertaining."

"I don't agree with you, but I accept that challenge," Mrik said. "I'm sure I will have plenty of time on the journey for a metamorphosis."

Pamatrical

Every time Mrik saw the Pamatrical, he was impressed. It is one of the most ornate buildings in all Arzola. Its exterior walls are two stories of immense statues of Arzolan heroes, with grandeur warranted by the memories of their entire civilization. It houses the virtual lives of all inhabitants of Arzola for the past 712 years.

As he prepared to meet his third great-grandfather for the first time, Mrik was still recovering from the celebration the previous night with Arlam and the Zeposze. Celebrations with the Zeposze were always enthusiastic. They had stayed close since childhood. Their parents all lived past the last tuble stop outside the town of Ciles. It is isolated, and so as children formed a close bond. Using their priboards to connect, they were always on them. Arlam and Mrik led the Zeposze on the priboards and had fun adjusting the small pyramid-shaped gravimags on the bottoms. They looked for exciting priboard adventures, and in Kufina they were right next to the Wave. Mrik had heard of an adventure his third great-grandfather had taken off the Wave, so here he was at the Pamatrical to speak with him.

"Mrhonorix, it is an honor to be able to speak to you," Mrik said, addressing a lifelike image of his third great-grandfather.

Mrhonorix's virtual mind could access the Cowav to retrieve all the knowledge of their existence and live video to visualize the living, but he could not input to the Cowav. His virtual mind was alive, but his body was not. He could see and hear but not speak with the living, except for occasions like this, when he received a personal visit.

"I've been following you," Mrhonorix responded.

"There has not been much to follow. My greatest desire is to have a grand Militan life like yours and honor my family and all the Militan."

"That is a splendid goal. It is special for me that you have initiated this conversation. I have not spoken with someone from the present for many years. I have learned of your life from the Cowav, but something tells me there is more to you than what the Cowav shows me."

"I would like to think so, but nothing I can do will ever compare to all the adventures of your life."

"I remember those challenges, but following your adventures excites me."

"I am considering starting with an adventure you took. My father told me about your jump into Mysticwild. However, because I cannot access it in the Cowav, I am hoping you can tell me about your venture."

"Mysticwild is not your typical adventure. There are unknowns around every corner, and there's a high chance you will lose your life. I was just lucky to live through my adventure. One of my buddies and I were about your age when we tied parachutes on our backs and jumped without having any information at all.

"I can still remember the feeling of drifting off the Wave and looking down to see the trextus with their massive rear legs and monstrous heads that seemed to be totally filled with flesh-ripping incisors. I felt paralyzed before I even landed but was lucky and came down in a tree. My buddy was not so lucky. He ended up in a flat field, where he was exposed to the trextus. They grabbed him and tore him apart before I could even escape my parachute. Fortunately, they cannot climb trees and are heavy sleepers. I did see one ex-Arzolan in a tree house, but after I saw my friend grabbed by trextus, my only thought was getting back. I stayed in the tree until the trextus were asleep and made my way to the Wave. You cannot get a good view of the Wave from this side, but it is immense.

"Looking up from Mysticwild, it was like a mountain with a gigantic breaking wave at the top. It is easy to understand how it took the lifetime of this planet to create this mystical separation of the warm and cold sides. There was no way to climb the overhang of the Wave, so I climbed to the underside and spent a month digging through. The tunnel should still be there. It is located about one hundred yards clockwise from the Blue Rock, which you can see from Mysticwild. However, after I used the tunnel, it was located, and a door was placed on it that can only be opened from this side. Nobody knew we were going, and I struggled with my friend's death. We were young and adventurous. I would not suggest this quest to anyone."

"I have never been in a life-or-death situation. Perhaps it is time. I aspire to have a great life like yours, so when I get here after my two hundred years, I will feel I have done my part as a member of the great Militan heritage."

"On your upcoming ten-year journey, you will probably experience life-or-death situations. Death is one resolution to life, but I think the virtual existence this Pamatrical provides is a better one. I watch life through the Cowav, and because I am a Militan, I see the part I played in the one thousand and thirty-six years of our traditions. Life here in the Pamatrical does not compare with living, but there is no stress or physical ailments. You should consider the part you play in our Militan heritage family before you cast your life out to risk without cause."

"If I cannot go into the unknown dangers of Mysticwild and survive, then I am not worthy of the ranks of the Militan warriors. But your thoughts on the risk will bear heavy on my decision. What advice can you give me, should I choose to take this adventure?"

"You are young and will have many opportunities to prove your valor. I do not think this should be one of them, but if you must go, you will need to control your fear but also listen to it."

"I have learned to block my fear as part of my quest to be a great Militan but have experienced the anxiety it creates."

"Your desire for adventure reminds me of my stash of millium. On one of my adventures we landed on an unknown planet. It was an exceptional experience, starting with the welcome celebration where everyone eat some millium. Millium is made from a beautiful purple flower and has a mind-expanding meander effect, which loosens your mind and creates freedom to untangle your thoughts. It stimulated a great friendship, and so I brought some back. I forgot to follow certain procedures in bringing it home to Arzola, and so I just hid it and drew a map to where it was. It is in an isolated location, and so I doubt that it has been disturbed. Here is the map.---It is all yours, if you would like."

"I am honored that you would entrust me with this valuable item. I will use the map to secure the millium and experience it on my ten-year adventure."

"Mrik, there is a task of much more consequence that I would like to entrust to you. It would benefit all Arzola. The other members of the Pamatrical and I have noticed inequalities developing in the Cowav. The Politan hereditary group has been gaining advantage, and the minorities, the Bruid and the Rollum, are losing. We have not told anyone of our observations, because we cannot communicate with the living except when we receive visits like this, and we are concerned who we report it to, since we don't know who is involved."

Mrhonorix paused, collected his thoughts, and continued, "The inequalities appear as a ripple in the Cowav, which indicates that there is a force that is pushing for a superior position. If the ripple grows, it would strike at the core of the Cowav and our mutual way of life. For the Cowav to exist we all must value the lives of everyone else the same as our own. Even though our mutual living goes against our basic genetic instinct, we have been able to master this for the past five hundred and seventy-six years.

"We have not been able to isolate this ripple," Mrhonorix explained. "However, if it continues, it could destroy the Cowav. There are seven hundred and twelve years of virtual Arzolan lives here in the Pamatrical. Our digital lives depend on the Cowav for our existence. When I received your request for a visit, I spoke with our Pamatrical Cenate, and we decided you were the person we wanted to trust with our existence. Once you start your journey, the Empyramis Cowav will be separate from the Arzola Cowav. We would like you to learn about this threat by identifying the ripple in the Empyramis Cowav. Then when you come back, we will know how to eliminate it from the Arzola Cowav."

Mrik looked directly into Mrhonorix's eyes and took a long breath. "I am surprised to learn of this ripple in the Cowav but honored that the Pamatrical Cenate has faith in me for this challenging mission. I will begin and gradually enlist my trusted friends for assistance. Do you have any leads?"

"The number of Politan accepted on your ten-year journey is twenty percent more than anyone else, and the Biru and the Rollum accepted twenty-five percent less than everyone else. That is just one example of how it would appear that the Politan have some sort of illicit control over the Cowav. Your main task will be to find out how they are manipulating the Cowav."

"Do you believe the Politan are behind this ripple?"

"All the information we have gathered has led us to that conclusion."

"I will report back to you as soon as I return."

Tuble Geyser

The geyser at Kufina is the biggest on the planet, and the air flows are extreme. Air exhaust from the Tuble transportation system generates the geyser. The air stream shoots straight up, creating a great launch for priboarders. Only the best priboarders even attempt to ride it and it takes some time to figure out the currents. Arlam and Mrik had always wanted to try it, but this was their first opportunity. There were a few other priboarders this morning, but the geyser was large enough to accommodate all of them. Mrik jumped in but was not perfectly balanced on his priboard and a strong burst of the tuble exhaust quickly tossed him sideways. He was out of the geyser and tumbled headfirst into the bushes around it. Arlam followed him into the geyser but fared no better and quickly plunged down beside Mrik.

"Well, at least I have an excuse," Arlam said. "I am still recovering from my game."

He was right, and Mrik was glad there were not many priboarders around, so he remained unnoticed as he prepared for his second attempt.

The second time he made sure he was perfectly centered and zoomed up until he got a little too self-confident and was again thrown out. This time Mrik was able to open his priboard wings just in time to make a secure, although not graceful, landing. Arlam crashed again and looked sheepishly toward Mrik. This was not their usual ride, and they could tell that most of the riders were regulars. They made it all the way to the top with a long, gradual glide down. Mrik did not feel good as a Militan, older than most of the riders and struggling to maintain his self-esteem, but he was not deterred. His third ride did not look beautiful, but at least he was able to make it to the top and back down.

"Where did you get that Priboard?" he asked Arlam.

"I customized it. I took two of the ten pyramid gravimags off the bottom. It is harder to stabilize, but it's easier to turn."

"Do you know that Politan that just did a flip?"

"No, but I can see why she caught your eye."

A couple of jumps later, Mrik leaped right after her and glided to where she landed to begin a conversation. He was particularly curious after what Mrhonorix had said about the Politan. Maybe he could get a feel for the advantage the Politan are trying to gain. But then she looked straight into his eyes as if to ask him what he is about. Mrik returned her gaze. He did not see anything related to a ripple, but he did see a heavy dose of intrigue.

"You have good balance. Didn't I see you at the Sisual Orb yesterday?" he asked.

"My balance is from superlative legs. I was at the Sisual Orb yesterday---it was a good game," she responded. "I'm just getting a few glides in before my flight on the Empyramis."

"I am on that flight also. How did you develop your great priboarding skill?"

"I guess you could say I did not like hanging with the group when I was growing up and spent a lot of time by myself on my priboard."

"That is opposite from me. I grew up with a group, and priboarding was all we did."

None of the Zeposze are part of the Politan hereditary order, and Mrik had never had a close relationship with a Politan. If he spent some time getting to know her, it would be a good first step in his new quest to find the cause of the Cowav ripple. After listening to Mrhonorix, he was thinking the Mysticwild adventure would not be a good idea.

However, it might provide the perfect excuse to get to know and establish a relationship with a Politan, so he asked her, "You are so skilled. How about gliding off the Wave with me before our flight?"

She frowned. "I thought that was an area out of our Cowav zone and not safe."

"That's true, but nowhere does it actually say it is prohibited."

"Okay, considering as a Militan you must have this all thought out and well planned, I will consider this little adventure before our journey. Where and when would I meet you if I decide to jump with you?"

"Well, I had not really worked out the details. However, as I want to get back for the national sisual championship, if we depart in two days, that will leave us three days, and we will still be back one day prior to the game and three days prior to the flight. Let's jump from the orange stone at first light."

On Mrik's next ride, he landed next to Arlam, who was now making it to the top of the geyser.

"Arlam, I'm going on an adventure with that gliding Politan."

"Wow, that was a fast connection. What is the adventure?"

"We are gliding off the Wave. Can you come with us?"

"Are you crazy? Of the few that have done that, fewer have returned."

"Maybe it is just so nice, no one wants to return."

"I don't think living in Mysticwild is something anyone would desire. Are you sure she agreed?"

"Well, she is considering."

"I would expect a no-show."

"I'm sure you are right, but I had not made up my mind yet, and now I no longer have a choice. I have to be there in two days so I have time to get back to see your game."

"Okay, what is the time and location? I want to see this flight."

"It's first light at the orange rock in two days."

Pre-Lift-Off

The Empyramis is new and massive. Its pyramid shape is similar to all previous Arzolan journey ships but is bigger. It replicates the environment on Arzola with a Teratura, which feels like a forest and garden combined---a Relux area for social interaction and an Xpys for physical activities. It would be their home for a decade, and Arlam and Mrik were attending the pre-takeoff celebration aboard the Empyramis.

"I guess they want to give us some information about last preparations," Arlam said.

"I don't know why they did not just post the information in the Cowav," Mrik responded.

"Everyone has gathered. Let's listen to your dad."

"We are spirits of adventure, creatures of time, minds of curiosity with hope of great fascinations. We will be traveling and living together for an exciting part of our lives. I will be steering us through a barrage of unknowns. You will research, explore, and enjoy this journey and come to know everyone because we are all family. Our ten-year journey will take us into the depths of our galaxy. We will be leaving some of you as visitors at three planets and adventuring beyond. Pradmiral will be our Noble One on our journey. He can provide mental awareness beyond the Cowav."

Pradmiral is one of the most respected Politans in Arzola, and he said a few words: "Activate life with me on this last of my journeys, and know that I am always ready for a game of Phi."

The captain continued, "As you carry on with your good-byes, know you have been chosen from all those who wished to journey with us because of your unique life. We will be creating a mini Arzola, and you have been selected to replicate as closely as possible our life on Arzola with all the excitement, adventure, stability, and security provided."

"Listening to your dad, I feel he will be a good captain," Arlam said. "Let's take a walk through this new Empyramis."

"Okay, but over there, I see the lady from the Tuble Geyser. Let's go say hello."

"Greetings, lady with the superlative legs." Mrik gave her a smile.

She nodded. "Greetings, gentleman of the priboard. This is my sister Psorephine, and I am Psozela."

"I am Mrik, and this is Arlam. Are you a superlative leg priboard glider like your sister?"

"Not hardly. Psozela has always taken her own path, and I have never been able to keep up with her."

"Are any other family members on this journey?"

"Our parents. However, they have passed their united years and are not together," Psorephine said.

"Have you toured this beautiful new ship?" Arlam asked.

"We were just thinking about how we should start touring the ship," Psorephine said.

"We are just on our way for a self-guided tour. Would you like to join us?" Mrik asked.

"Yes, we would," Psozela said. "As a Militan you must be part of the crew?"

"Yes, I am. I will be commanding one of the Trivac ships. Let's start at the bottom, at the landing deck. I will show you my Trivac ship."

The landing deck is a big open space with all the various ships surrounding the center, leaving room for launching and landing.

We had finished our walk around the deck when Psorephine said, "Wouldn't it be nice to go for a ride over the Arzola countryside before we leave?"

"What do you mean?" Mrik asked.

"As a Militan, can't you just jump in one of these ships and take off?" Psozela wanted to know.

"About the same way you as a Politan can enter the Cowav and change facts that do not benefit you," Mrik said.

He was hoping to egg her on a little to see if she would show any indication of support for the Cowav ripple. Those involved must be feeling a little pleased with their actions, creating a ripple without being noticed. There is always someone who cannot resist using that feeling of superiority to advance their own agenda. This would be the perfect time for her to show her ego. But there was nothing in her answer.

"Okay, I get your point. So, is there a way we can borrow one of these machines for a little joy ride to remember Arzola before we leave?" Psozela asked.

"That sounds like fun, but I don't even know if these ships are charged up yet," Mrik said.

"There is a nice little shuttle over there. Let's see if it is charged," Arlam said.

Mrik went along with Arlam's suggestion, thinking it would not be charged and that would be the end of the joy-riding desires. Unfortunately, it was charged, and now Mrik had to tell them that he had built his status as a Militan on making decisions that did not include joy-riding shuttles. They could not go for a ride, even though they all seemed to be excited about the prospect.

"There is nobody on the deck to see us," Psozela said, "and if they did, they would just think it was an authorized flight."

Arlam added, "If anyone were to catch us, we could say we thought a flight was just part of the Empyramis pre-lift-off open house."

"That might be fine for you, but they require better of me."

"What happened to that spirit of adventure you always carry around with you?"

"Okay," Mrik said, "but let's be back in thirty minutes, because the security system starts in two hours, and we would definitely be questioned if we are not back before then."

This was not typical behavior for any of them, but getting together on this special occasion must have sparked a streak of their youth and the desire for true excitement. Exploring the Empyramis was new, but they knew they would have ten years to do that, and a little joy ride was exciting. As a Militan and a member of the crew, Mrik was the one responsible, and he knew the Cowav and the captain would not approve. But he justified it as part of the Cowav ripple investigation, where he needed to develop relations with the Politan to find out what they are doing. Psozela and Psorephine could be good representatives, although Mrik would hate to think of them as wanting to hurt their mutual way of life.

They escaped unnoticed. The view of the countryside was great, and they were enjoying the feelings, like when they were kids and figured out how to skip school for a day of priboarding.

"Let's head for the other side of that ridge so we'll be out of sight and then see what this baby can do," Arlam said.

"Strap in," Mrik said. "This honey has the new defensive twist motion."

He quickly thrust us up and into a triple twisting rollover. It was so fast it was hard to keep his direction, but the automatic backup was with him the whole way as he finished the rollover and started the zig-zag jumps. Arlam, Psozela, and Psorephine were just hanging on until the end of the jumps, when Arlam said, "I guess you can still fly."

"Psozela, take controls," Mrik said.

"Sure, but Politans are leaders, not flyers," Psozela said.

"Yes, but what do you lead?"

"We lead idiots like you that max out a little shuttle just to try and impress a couple of Politans."

Mrik was trying to continue the conversation in the hope she would lose her train of thought and slip something that might expose some part of the ripple.

"I know a place just on the other side of that hill that has some good wild polusos berries," Psozela said.

"I know a great recipe for polusos berry hlyusir," Mrik said, "and it is a beautiful day for picking. But we must be back before the security watch starts."

They landed gently, grabbed some helmets hanging in the shuttle, which would make do for berry baskets, and headed out to the thorny polusos brambles to begin picking.

"Did you enjoy growing up in the countryside of Ciles?" Psozela asked Mrik.

His first thought was, *She remembered where I lived.* It was a sign of interest, which created a bit of delight.

"It was all I knew, but we had a group and called ourselves the Zeposze, and we were always doing things together, and we never lacked for excitement. How did you like growing up in the big city?" Mrik asked.

"I was mostly by myself, but the area was so diverse that I always had new and interesting experiences."

"Are you glad you were born a Politan?"

"It is what I am, what I will always be. I guess I am pleased I am not a Militan."

"I was thinking the rather formal structure of the Politan would be something that might be divergent from your lifestyle."

"They tolerate me, and that is good enough for me. How do you deal with the structure and rigors of the Militan?"

"It makes life easy. I just follow what I need to, and then I have all the rest of my time to exercise my own freedom." Mrik dropped a handful of berries into the helmet then reached to pick more. "How did you end up getting accepted for the Journey?" he asked.

"My mother signed on as a Politan official and encouraged me to go. I'm getting close to uniting age and wanted to have a little adventure."

It was a beautiful day for picking polusos berries, but they had to limit their enjoyment and head back to the Empyramis, where they were able to slip into the landing area without notice.

"Well, that was an exciting ride," Psorephine said.

Psozela turned to Mrik and asked, "It seems like the jump you are making tomorrow would be a great self-risk. What is your benefit?"

"No benefit, but an adventure," he said.

"Are you prepared for the morning?"

"I think so. I will wait for you till first light plus ten."

As Psozela listened to him, she was hesitant about journeying to Mysticwild. She knew little about it, but the intrigue of venturing into the unknown with this Militan, who had the physique and stature of a skymaster, gave her chills of excitement and anticipation of the possibilities of a relationship, the nature of which she had not experienced.

Standing on the Wave

The sun was just starting to reflect off the far distant trees over the Wave. The wind howled across the precipice at the top of this boundary between the warm and cold sides. Mrik stood with Arlam, mulling his decision to take flight into the midst of the perilous side of the planet. Mysticwild lived only in the stories carried in conversation outside the Cowav. The perpendicular rotation of Arzola to its sun left one side of the planet warm and the other side cold and, in the middle, where the wind blew from the warm to cold, soil accumulated like a mountain range with a wave at the crest. It extended the full circumference of the planet and was truly mystical.

Mrik had reviewed the risks involved. He had heard the stories claiming only half of those that ventured beyond the Wave ever return, but he wondered if the half that had not returned were still there living an enjoyable life. He didn't think he would make this adventure, but he had committed to that Politan, and he could not pass on the opportunity to start working on his task for Mrhonorix to locate the source and content of the Cowav ripple.

The winds were strongest at the peak but unknown on the other side because of the great elevation drop. As Mrik stood with Arlam and gazed over the Wave, he could not help but wonder if a flight into this vast unknown would end his life and possibly the life of a trusting Politan. Although he had done some risky adventures in my past, none compare with this flight into such a land of mystery and foreboding. From the crest he could only see the distant green horizon, but he knew that just below was the land of the trextus.

The biggest risk was the unknown. Mrik did not understand why information on this half of the planet was the only thing not referenced in the Cowav. He had learned with his first teachings it is forsaken territory, but no reason was given. The absence of information was like an open invitation to his curious mind, looking to fill the void he could not fill without this perilous adventure.

"The trextus are just waiting for you," Arlam said, "and although you may feel excited about having to do battle with one of the most aggressive and nasty creatures, your story may never get told. I can think of better ways to give your life. This Wave is nature telling us there is a separation here and observance of this separation is fated. However, if you must do this adventure, I will check at the tunnel door, every day at high sun. But please consider---your decision is not made until you jump. This could be the last jump you ever make. I think you need to take a break and step back from the edge. It is not too late to change your mind. There must be a reason why it is forsaken."

"It's just those unknown characteristics that make it intriguing. Every other part of life I have instant access to through the Cowav, but imagine what is out there. The adventure is pure. But I am still thinking, and if at the last moment I step back from the edge, you will know I have listened to your advice."

"Someone is coming. Better hide your flight equipment."

"Wait---it is Psozela. I did not think she was seriously considering, but there is no mistaking her."

When Psozela moved, the slight sway of her hips spawned an almost indistinguishable motion that stirred excitement. Her sway was so delicate, it was pretty to watch and yet so natural to her. She always seemed to wear stunning clothes that left exposed a little of the short, smooth, soft, and sensual mint green fur that covered her back with stripes of harvest wheat colors. Her self-confidence reflected a natural charisma, probably coming from those stripes that originated millions of years ago, when the Arzolans were not in control of their environment and scampered through the grasses to escape predators.

"Greetings, Psozela. Arlam has just summarized all the reasons why I should not take this adventure. Should he repeat them for you?"

Psozela responded, "No. I already know this is not an intelligent decision, yet here I stand."

"My third great-grandfather, Mrhonorix, told me the warm currents coming off the edge should give us good lift, but we need to make it to the trees. If we land in the plains the trextus will see us coming and be after us right away. This is your chance to skip this adventure. Our Cowav won't be working, and if we don't make it back for the flight---well, that's a mess."

"You're not going to scare me. Have you checked your priboard wings for tension? Do you have your supply of nutrients? Have you talked to the Sage?"

"Yes, and the Sage told me life after is only relevant to those who have an empty space to fill."

"The Sage told me to adventure with the strength of the opposition. I took that to mean it was not going to be easy."

"Arlam, this is goodbye. We will see you at the tunnel door one day soon. We plan to be back in time to see your game."

Arlam clapped a hand on my shoulder. "Just get back any way you can. I will be waiting at high sun each day at the door."

"Follow me back far enough so I don't interfere with your lift," Mrik said as Psozela tightened her straps. "But remember, you need to be close enough so we can both end up in the same area. On three. One, two, three."

Mysticwild

Mrik jumped and dropped quickly. Psozela knew she must jump. She did not expect this much turbulence. Mrik was way ahead. She must make up some ground. There was a trextus—horrific! She was going to die. Her mind flashed her whole life as if in a living dream, from her childhood through meeting Mrik. She had lived a good life. She would not have lived it any other way. Her lifestyle had always put her at risk, and it finally caught up with her. Her family and friends would understand. She hoped the trextus would make it quick. Maybe she could dip and pick up some speed. There was a thermal over there that should get her back up. A little breeze—if she could just make it over to those trees, maybe she could survive. She was missing the Cowav already. It looked like Mrik was headed for that clearing next to the trees. She should be able to catch the edge.

Hard landing but still alive. The plants were really tall. She hoped Mrik would stay where he landed so she could find him.

A rattling in the bush—Mrik sure got there quick. Wait. Oh, it was not Mrik.

An Arzola-looking being appeared and said, "Don't be afraid. Follow me—we must move quickly. The trextus will be following you and be here shortly. We must find your friend and get to the trees."

Psozela was thinking, *He looks like an Arzolan and speaks our language.* Without a lot of options, she was inclined to

20

think he was friendly, and so she followed. Mrik was coming their way when they met him.

Psozela's new friend said to Mrik, "I am your only hope here in trextus land. Follow me to the trees."

Mrik responded, "Who are you?"

"I am Pralosma. I can lead you from the immediate danger. Come with me if you want. I am leaving now."

Pralosma lived in a tree house in the top of a great tree. He saw us coming. Mrik and Psozela followed him.

"We are safe here," Pralosma said. "Why have you ventured over the Wave?"

Mrik responded, "We wanted to experience this side of the planet."

"You are lucky I saw you. The trextus were about to give you an experience of Mysticwild, but not the type you were looking for."

"Thank you for your assistance. Why did you come over the Wave?" Psozela asked.

"I needed to get away."

"What were you escaping from?"

"On the warm side I could see my whole life. Here my life is unknown. I live day to day and am completely self-reliant. There are plenty of great trees here for house building, if you would like to join us."

Mrik responded, "That sounds intriguing, but we want to be back in two days for the national sisual championship."

"Well, you better start thinking about your return, because it will probably take you three days if you leave in the morning."

Psozela asked, "Why will it take so long, when you can see the Wave from here?"

"The only way back to the warm side is through the Wave. The only way through the Wave is a tunnel, which I have heard about but not actually seen. It is apparently close to where you jumped, but the territory between here and there is trextus territory, and you would only be a tasty snack for them. The less risky way to get there is to take the

Mirudian River through the Jagger Jungle, the narrow rapids and over the waterfalls, then glide to the edge of the Wave and climb the curve of the Wave until you are out of the reach of the trextus. Then you can look for the tunnel.

"But enough of that for now. I will brief you on what you need to know later. Now please make yourselves at home while I contact the locals so we can have a celebration of our new guests. It has been eight years since our last visitor from the warm side, and he is still here."

While Pralosma was making his contacts, Mrik said, "I think we should wait for nightfall and then head through the trextus territory so we can get back to see Arlam's championship game. Mrhonorix said the trextus are heavy sleepers, and if we hurried, we should make it by first light."

"Did you not see those trextus?" Psozela asked. "Do you know how to keep from stumbling on them as you cross their territory in the dark? And how does Mrhonorix in his few hours in Mysticwild know more than these locals? Let's not make this priboard adventure of yours more life-threatening than it already is."

"You are probably right. Let's go with the locals."

"Did you notice that Pralosma kept his name? So, he must have been a Politan with his first letter a 'P' and the second letter 'r,' indicating male. We should be able to identify the hereditary order of any Arzolans that are here, even though they will not be wearing their hereditary toppers."

Sryber and Rrholer were the first to arrive, and right away Sryber was offering us some of his myrita hlyusir and telling us how he makes this special drink with myrita berries and a little of his special concoction.

"What is the effect of your myrita hlyusir?" Psozela asked.

"It will loosen your mind so you can experience the allure of Mysticwild," he said.

"Is that why you came to Mysticwild, to loosen your mind?" I asked.

"Actually, when I was still on the warm side, I did some research and altered a gene in a plant so it could signal when it needed water. The Cowav decided it could not allow such change because it was not natural, so I decided to go somewhere I could use my creativity and found myself here."

Rrholer, who had lived his whole life in Mysticwild, asked, "Why do you wear fancy things on your body?"

Rrholer was a rollum, a circular being with a body like a snake. They can wrap their tails to their heads to form a circle so they can roll, using their two small legs and arms to push off.

"You mean like this sunfus?"

"Yes."

"It is meant to look pleasing and attract attention."

"Attention is something you don't want to attract here, where the trextus are always on the prowl."

"What is it like living here with the trextus?" Psozela asked.

"The trextus know they can't catch me when I'm rolling, and as long as I don't venture into the cold areas, life is pretty mellow. Plenty of food, and everyone is friendly."

Pop, who also lived his whole life in Mysticwild, entered and quickly said, "Tell me about your life above the Wave."

"We have rollums like Rrholer on our side of the planet, but I have never seen a species like you," Psozela said.

Pop's body looked like it is made of two balls, a big one at the bottom and a smaller one at the top, all covered and joined with a layer of fuzzy green hair that looks like it had evolved to blend in with the local vegetation. His legs and arms gave him sufficient mobility but would not give him the agility to do well playing sisual.

Mrik was still taking in the surroundings but answered Pop's question. "Everyone is part of the Cowav, which supports our mutual way of life, where everyone treats everyone else the same way they treat themselves. No trextus or anything like them."

Mrik as a Militan was used to everything ordered and understood. Psozela sensed this environment left him concerned. I think Pop also sensed this.

"Mrik have you ever played Phi?" Pop asked.

"Yes."

"Well, let's see if you are any good."

As Mrik sat down to play, another apparent ex-Arzolan came in and straight over to talk to me.

"Greetings," she said, "and welcome to Mysticwild. I see you have some of Sryber's special myrita hlyusir, so you should be ready to tell your story of why you came over the Wave."

"Well, I thought it was going to be a little priboard adventure before I go on a ten-year interstellar trip, but I had no idea what I was getting into. Tell me about your life here in Mysticwild. How long have you been here?" Psozela asked.

"I flew off the edge thirty years ago. I was young and thought the stringent, formal way of the Cowav was not the best possible life. I spent a couple years adapting to this way of existence and trying to understand this new reality. After I figured out that the Cowav wasn't so bad, I had established my life here and wasn't sure I could make it back in the Cowav."

"Doesn't it get lonely here?"

"I have my close friends right here and other ex-Arzolans scattered around. There is a common site where everyone meets, every triple moon. We party and discuss predators. As long as we stay out of the trextus territory, it is peaceful and mellow."

"Okay, everyone," Pralosma said to get the group's attention. "It is time to make a plan for getting these two back to the warm side. With the limited time they have, I think the only way is to take the Mirudian River. If they use their priboards and jump off the top of the falls, they should be able to make it to the area of the tunnel and above the reach of the trextus."

"The problems will be getting them into the Jagger Jungle and through the narrow rapids," Pop said. "The trextus have been sleeping at the entrance to the Jagger Jungle, and they always watch the narrow rapids."

Rrholer, having grown up with the trextus, said, "I will create a distraction to draw them away from the Jagger Jungle entrance, but the narrow rapids will not be as easy. The trextus like to congregate there, and once you start down the river, you cannot stop without great risk."

"We will need to build a raft," Pralosma said. "Let's meet here tomorrow so Rrholer can distract the trextus and we can get into the Jagger Jungle and build a raft."

Pralosma brought out some weapons and body paint camouflage. "Here are some weapons you might want to take with you. You do not want anything that will restrict your movement, but there are many unknowns along your path that will take advantage of any vulnerability you may have. Here also is some body paint. A little camouflage could make a big difference in your passage."

While Mrik was looking through the weapons, Psozela was checking out the body paint.

"Mrik, what do you think of my camouflage?"

"The rose is very sensual; of course, so is the leg it is painted on."

"The foot on the end of that sensual leg is going to smack your head if you do not get your mind back into our mission. Have you found out the advantages of the different weapons?"

"It's hard to know the dangers ahead, but I think we should each take one of these long and slender but strong swords and one rope. We will also have our small personal knives we brought with us."

"Give me my sword. I will strap it to my back in the morning."

The rest of the evening was a pleasant exchange of life experiences from two different worlds, fueled by the enjoyable myrita hlyusir.

Morning came, and they started. Rrholer allowed his appearance to be seen by the trextus, who immediately pursued him. Rrholer rolled up and rolled off on this predetermined path, which drew the trextus away from the others. They scampered into the Jagger Jungle with the supplies and got busy building the raft.

Pralosma gave them a clue as to what to expect. "It should be easy floating through the Jagger Jungle. Just stay in the center and watch for things hanging from branches above, and make sure you are in the center when you come out of the Jungle. The trextus watch the river at that point. They cannot reach the center, but they like to throw rocks. I am putting three spears on the raft in case the trextus get close. When you get to the narrow rapids, you will be exposed. You can go off-center as needed, but do not get too close to either side, where trextus may be waiting. After you get through the narrow rapids you will float for a while, but you must be ready with your priboards when you get to the waterfall. As soon as you go over the waterfall, you must jump from the raft.

"Look for the Blue Rock. It stands out among the vegetation and is said to mark the approximate location of the tunnel. The wind should be at your back, but if you start falling too fast, make sure you get to the Wave and high enough to be out of the reach of the trextus. They are not good climbers."

"I'm going to go with you part of the way," Pop said. "I am the only one that can get off the raft without going to shore. We will need torches to light our travel tonight in the jungle."

There was not a lot of light for building a raft in the Jagger Jungle even in daylight, but with all the help they were able to finish while it was still light.

Pop, Mrik and Psozela I loaded the raft with their weapons and some quickly put-together shields. Lush vegetation surrounded the river, as if it were running through a tunnel, but the branches on the inside were barren. They could stand up and touch the branches, but the water was not high, and floating down the river was not a problem.

After spending a couple of hours on the river, night came, and they lit the torches.

Psozela relaxed a little as they meandered down the river, and then she confronted Mrik. "What did you get me involved in?"

Mrik responded, "What did I get you involved in? When you arrived at the Wave, I was surprised. I was planning on taking Arlam's advice when you came, but I could not turn back once you said you were ready to go."

"But this is not the priboard flight into the unknown I was expecting. Didn't you do any research on this place?"

"You know the Cowav contains no information on Mysticwild. There was nothing to find other than what I learned from Mrhonorix."

"Well, if we get out of this, I will know the stupid mentality of the Militan."

Then just as Psozela was turning around to make her point more emphatic, she heard a frightening scream from Mrik and saw Pop fly off the raft. Something had latched onto Mrik's arm, and in trying to encircle him had knocked Pop off the raft with its tail or some part of its body. Psozela quickly grabbed her knife and started to stab at its body, but it kept entangling Mrik. So she gave the knife to Mrik, who had one hand free, but the creature forced him to the edge of the raft in an attempt to get him in the water. Psozela grabbed the spear and went for its head. She got a good hit just as they tumbled off the raft.

Psozela followed them in, and it became a tussle with Mrik and her against this creature. Mrik was trying to cut the tentacle that was holding him, and Psozela was stabbing at its head. The river was too deep to stand, and so it was a struggle to get a breath. Suddenly the creature loosened and was gone. Psozela should have been ecstatic, but all she could think about was getting back on the raft. Mrik was close, and although he was favoring one arm, he was able to stay afloat. The raft had continued down the river, but Pop popped back on and was slowing it down. Mrik was struggling with his hurt arm but was more concerned with getting Psozela back on the raft than himself.

They both got on safely and took care of punctures to Mrik's arm. Then they laid flat on their backs, watching every inch of the ceiling above them. Pop said an attack by a bazcum was unusual, but then he could not remember the last time he had ventured through the Jagger Jungle on the Mirudian River.

We had spent one night and part of a day in the Jagger Jungle when Pop said, "We are coming to the end of the jungle. Let's get to the center of the river and prepare ourselves for the daylight."

Mrik whispered, "I see two trextus on the right side."

Psozela mentioned the one she saw on the left. "He has seen us and is getting excited. He is throwing rocks."

Pop said, "They do not have much of a throwing arm, but keep an eye out for anything that might come close."

Mrik observed, "It looks like one just jumped into the water."

Pop turned to see him and said, "They are not known to be swimmers, but we better get our spears ready in case he gets close. Let's paddle—maybe we can outrun him."

Mrik took on his Militan role and started directing them. "He is making it. Pop, watch for rocks. Psozela and I will try and keep this trextus at bay with our spears. Psozela, go for his mouth, and I'll try for an eye."

Fortunately, he is not a good swimmer. Psozela missed his mouth, but he winced from her spear in the side of his face. Mrik missed his eye but hit his ear.

The trextus's upper appendages are short and not used much; consequently they are weak, so when he grabbed the raft with one hand, it was not secure. Both Mrik and Psozela speared it at the same time, and that did it for the trextus.

Pop observed, "It looks like he decided we are not worth the effort. Good work with the spears."

With the immediate threat gone, they had clear floating and time to look around. The crystal-clear water was peaceful, with splotches of purple- and yellow-petaled flowers on the shoreline and in higher areas. Tall green reeds crowded the lower areas between the flowers. Forests of giant trees were in the background, watching over everything. The Wave, running the full length of the horizon, was visible in the far distance. Pop was telling stories of his growing up in Mysticwild. He really enjoyed popping around, and the trextus didn't seem to bother him. But now the rapids were approaching, and they were going to be perilously close to the edges, where the trextus like to hang out. They hid behind the shields, hoping they would not be noticed. They let the river take them but steered back to the center whenever they drifted off course.

"Make sure you are tied to the raft," Pop said. "It will get rough, and with the trextus grabbing at us, it will be easy to lose our footing."

"I can see them on either side of the rapids, and they see us. There is one leaning from the right."

Pop said, "They are afraid of the rapids, but they will try and grab us as we go by."

"It looks like that little one is winking at me. Now he is climbing on the back of that big one and jumping. Look out."

They all grabbed on to the raft as a swell of water splashed over and pushed them toward the other side and away from the little one. They started to paddle back to the center, but one trextus was able to grab ahold of the shield that Mrik was using. Mrik struggled with the vastly stronger trextus, but the trextus had unstable footing and a limited grip on the shield. Psozela quickly grabbed the spear and went for his hand. He let go with the hand she hit but was still able to hang on with the other.

Mrik was resisting being pulled off the raft with his feet, which were grabbing the end log of the raft. But this was causing the raft to stop as other trextus rush to join. Psozela quickly thrust the spear toward the other hand. She got a good hit, and the trextus released, which gave them a thrust away from the side and toward the center. They used their spears to deter the other trextus as the raft drifted back toward the center of the rapids. The rapids were relaxing and the river widening, and it seemed to have discouraged the trextus, giving them a chance to exhale.

"You are quite handy with that spear," Mrik said.

"I'm glad you had the shield. That trextus was really intent on getting at us," Psozela said.

"You are the first Politan that I have really gotten to know. I guess not all Politans are aloof from the rest of Arzola."

"No more than all Militans are strict disciplinarians."

"Are there groups of Politans that you spend your time with?"

"No, I like to do my own thing, and in Kufina the hereditary orders are more intermingled than in the smaller towns. I spend a lot of my time creating new acquaintances."

"I have not had the wide range of acquaintances as you in the big city, but I have found that the Biru and Rollum do not have the same level of civility as the Holua."

"I'm surprised at your observation. I have good friends that are Biru and Rollum, and I have felt that the Biru have an intellectual ability that is greater than the Holua, and the Rollum have always shown a greater emotional awareness than the Holua."

"It is probably just my limited exposure from my small-town background."

The conversation seemed a little strange, but Psozela could not help but like this strong but considerate man. She was sure glad he was with her, going through the narrow rapids.

After another day of floating down the river, Pop said, "See that big tree on the left? That tree marks the line of the waterfall. I am leaving now to give you room to prepare your priboards. You have shown me an adventure I will never forget, and I will always hope someday, somewhere I will see you again."

Mrik responded, "Thank you for everything, and particularly your friendship."

Psozela give Pop a big hug, not knowing if it even had any meaning to him.

A big pop out of Pop's rear end propelled him to shore, where he turned for a quick wave and scampered into the tall reeds.

As the raft went off the edge of the waterfall, Psozela and Mrik jumped. Mrik had trouble with his wingspan, but then recovered below her, so she dropped to his level.

Mrik used cerebral wave to communicate. #I lost us some height, but we have a good current. That must be the Blue Rock over there. Let's try the current in closer to the Wave—there should be some updraft.#

Psozela hoped Mrik knew where he was going, because that trextus under her looked like he was licking his chops.

Mrik yelled, "Land as high as you can. Climb straight up as quickly as possible."

As if he needed to tell her. That hurt—hard landing. Grab the board, and straight up. Mrik already scampering up. He was looking back to check on Psozela.

"Quick," he said, "the trextus are coming. I don't know how high they can go. Grab the tree roots."

At this point Psozela was not even taking the time to look back at the trextus—she was just scampering for her life. She could hear some heavy breathing behind her that did not sound far off. It was hard to get a good foothold, so she welcomed Mrik's hand.

He said, "Keep going. I want to see if I can discourage them."

He threw his knife and hit the first trextus in the eye. That trextus fell back, but there was another one right behind him. However, it gave them a little time, and Psozela and Mrik were starting to get up on the Wave. She paused to check on Mrik, but he said, "Don't look—just go fast."

She keep climbing but must have been getting out of trextus range. She came to a place where she must decide on a direction. They both stopped and turned around and could see the trextus. Apparently, the two of them were above the trextus' climbing range. They were now throwing stones, but they didn't have Arlam's throwing arm.

"Which way now?" Psozela asked Mrik.

Mrik said, "Mrhonorix told me it is one hundred lengths clockwise from the Blue Rock. We are about one hundred lengths clockwise now. Since we cannot go straight up, we must choose right or left. If I were going to build a tunnel, I would take the easiest way up. Left has more gradual rock. Let's go left."

"I will lead. 'Gradual' sounds good to me."

"Wait, what is over there? It looks like a slag pile."

Psozela turned to see where he was pointing and saw joy on his face—maybe the first time she had seen something reminiscent of a smile since they had jumped the Wave.

Mrik took off his sword and headed straight into the tunnel. A few minutes later he was back out.

"It is a really small tunnel, but I did make it to the door," Mrik said. "Now all we have to do is spend the night and knock at the door at high sun tomorrow. There is a flat space dug out of the hillside. Probably made by Mrhonorix. It is big enough for one person. We can dig it out for both of us or find a second bed."

"Your day's activities have probably frazzled you, so I guess it would be good to give you some warmth tonight. Let's make this area a little bigger."

Shortly before high sun, Mrik entered the tunnel. It is only big enough for one person, and so Psozela waited. After about thirty minutes, he emerged from the tunnel. "Nothing," he said. "I knocked and knocked, but the door did not open."

"This is not good." Psozela felt her brow crease. "What do we do now?"

"I can't believe Arlam was not there. Either he had some calamity, or there is another tunnel."

"We have to consider the fact Arlam might not arrive," I said.

"A depressing thought, leaving us with three options. One is to dig around the door's safety grid, which extends for an unknown radius. A second option is to look for a second tunnel in case that is where Arlam is. The third option is to dig a new tunnel."

"Let's start by working on all three options," Psozela said. "I will go in and start digging a tunnel to the edge of the safety grid. You can search for another existing tunnel or a place that would be good for us to dig a new tunnel. Be back here in an hour, and we will trade positions."

Claustrophobia is not a good feeling, but missing the flight would be life-changing. Psozela was able to make it through her hour. Mrik was back when she emerged from the tunnel.

"What did you find?" she asked.

"Nothing. I will start digging, and you can look for a second tunnel in the opposite direction. Maybe we will get lucky," Mrik said.

She headed out on her quest but had to pay attention, because the trextus were just waiting for her to lose her step. She was just glad she was out of their throwing range. When she got back, Mrik was just coming out of the tunnel.

"Did you run into any rocks?" she asked.

"No, but it sure is slow digging with just one knife."

"I found a place that might be the best alternative for a new tunnel, but there is no way we could dig it in time to make the flight. I think we need to concentrate on getting around the safety grid."

"We can work together. One will dig while the other one removes dirt, and tonight one can dig while the other one sleeps."

They made it through the night and were close to midday.

Psozela reminded Mrik, "Don't forget to knock on the door at high sun."

It is about high sun when suddenly, she saw a bright light at the end of the tunnel and heard a celebratory yell from Mrik. Next, she heard him say, "Grab our stuff. We are done tunneling."

Arlam had opened the door. Psozela felt relief, and now on the last day possible, she knew they would make their flight.

Arlam with serious apologies said, "So sorry. We won the championship, and the celebration was like nothing I had ever seen. It felt like all Arzola turned out, and the party went on all night. I just got so consumed in the celebrations I totally forgot my high sun appointment. But you are back and safe, so all is well."

"I am going straight to my home to get ready for the lift-off party," Psozela said. "I will see you two there."

Oluviam Hall

Dazzling lights, dynamic sounds, and delightful celebration filled the Laximal Plaza as Arzolans from around the planet came to celebrate the lift-off of the Empyramis. Arzola has two ships, and there is a party before take-off every five years. Everyone is excited.

The party was at Oluviam Hall. The hall is circular, with rooms around the circumference that host each heritage order. It is part of the Laximal Plaza made up of the Pamatrical, the Sisual Orb, the Oluviam Hall, and the

Empyramis launching area. It is in the center of Kufina, and the lush green, natural vegetation tries to encroach on the Plaza, because all buildings except their homes and the Laximal Plaza are underground. The Laximal Plaza provides all of them an area to gather and feel their Arzolan pride.

The balcony is where the youth of the growing and learning year like to hang out. However, Mrik thought it would be a good spot to get an overview of any intriguing females. He was standing at the railing of the balcony when Mrlfectori came up to speak with him. Mrlfectori had met Mrik earlier. His dad was Mrbrixton, the second in command of the Empyramis. Mrlfectori was just getting to the age where his physical attraction to females was starting to enter his consciousness, and he figured Mrik might be a good mentor in his pursuit of understanding. Mrlfectori approached Mrik, knowing that as a fellow Militan, he would assist him in any way he could.

"Mrik," Mrlfectori said, "since you have joined the young ones on the balcony, I thought maybe you would convey some of your wisdom from your years of female encounters."

"Mrlfectori, finding your uniting partner is a big endeavor that will probably consume most of your thirty years of single life. If you are lucky, you will find a soul mate—a female that merges so well, you act as one. Until you find a soul mate, which may never happen, you will be looking for a female to create a special relationship, but while in pursuit, you want to enjoy all the new relationships you will be creating. The more contacts, the better."

"How do I create these contacts?" Mrlfectori asked.

"You can play relation games if it helps. To play a game you become someone different than you are. When I was young, I used to play games. Now I am just putting off the decision I will soon have to make. I used two approaches when I was gaming. One was, *I'm a Super Being*, and the other was, *This Is Who I Am*. When I played *Super Being*, I wanted them to believe I am of greater value to them so later they would seek me out. If I were to smile as in *This is Who I*

Am, then they probably would not have had the same desire to seek me out but felt more secure with me. It is a game, but an enjoyable game, and it's a way to learn what you need to know to find your best uniting partner. This should be an enjoyable part of your life, and getting to know many different females of all hereditary orders will be stimulating."

After speaking with Mrik, Mrlfectori wanted to exercise his new knowledge. He saw Psruzam and figured she would be perfect to try a little game playing with *I'm a Super Being.*

"Hi, Psruzam."

"Hello, Mrlfectori."

"Well, since we are going on this ten-year adventure together, let's talk eluva."

Psruzam responded, "Okay, Mrlfectori, what do you want to know?"

"I realize to make mysuvisx, a special eluva has to be created, but isn't the first-time celebration enough?"

"Pretty lame, Mrlfectori. The first time must be the most special of all. You have a lot to learn before you will ever get close to a girl."

"You know, Psruzam, there is a chance we won't make it back from this trip."

"Eighty-nine percent of all voyages return safely, and ten years may not give you enough time to create the extra sensational celebration you will need to persuade a girl to spend a precious experience with you. You should probably be looking for a Militan to have your experience with."

"I will unite with a Militan, but I want to experience the rhythm of life first."

"If you want to have an eluva you should be thinking about making it enjoyable for your partner first. A little blossom and mints will get you further than your inflated ego."

"I need my ego for my pursuit but will remember your desires for blossom and mints."

Back down on the first level of the Oluviam Hall, the celebration was joyous. Mrik saw Psozela as she walked in.

Mrik headed down, found Psozela, and said, "That is a unique topper. Looks like a Pop feather on top."

Psozela responded, "He gave it to me just before he popped off the raft."

"They are dancing in the lovation room," Psozela said as she grabbed Mrik's hand.

The room is tall and has rails and bars used to create imaginative dance motions. A lot of swinging and swirling. You could tell a couple had been dancing together when they had elegant catches and swings between bars as they stayed in beat with the music.

"I have not spent as much time dancing as I have priboarding," Mrik said. "I might need a little help flowing to the music."

"You just need to loosen your Militan muscles."

"It's not my muscles you must free up; it is my psyche."

"So, I need to tantalize your thoughts?"

"No, you need to make me feel like I can make a fool of myself and still have fun."

"You already made a fool of yourself inviting me to Mysticwild, so you should be ready for some fun. My fun is just knowing I am on this side of the tunnel and ready for the take-off."

"Let's start our dance with a little pop to remember our friend."

Lift-Off

The youth raced down the outside surface of the Empyramis in reckless abandon and yet seemed to emerge at the bottom unscathed.

The gravomagnetic waves coming off the surface of the Empyramis create a great place for priboarding, and the youth were taking advantage of their last morning on Arzola.

As the captain walked toward the Empyramis for final boarding, he could hear voices near the apex.

Mrlfectori and Mri, the two sons of Mrbrixton, and some of their new friends were priboard racing down the outside of the Empyramis. The captain was responsible, but they would not get another chance for a long time, so he accepted the risk of them getting bruised.

Their voice waves were pulsating down the slope of the Empyramis.

"Mri, watch—the bottom comes up quick," Mrlfectori said.

Mri, not wanting to acknowledge his younger age, responded, "Yah, it will come quicker for me."

Before another word could be said, they were racing down the surface of the ship and there as they hit the bottom—*slam*— Mri thumped into the textured take-off surface, unable to turn quickly enough.

Mrlfectori laughed as Mri pulled himself off the ground to say, "I may hurt, but I beat you."

Just as they were ready to start their second run, a blue light from the Priyramelo at the apex of the ship started flashing.

The captain signaled to the kids. They needed to prepare for their great adventure.

As he entered the Empyramis, he felt good. This would be his first flight as captain, but he had been preparing for the last ten years, and he was ready.

The plates in the exterior walls of the Empyramis and its pyramid shape amplify the gravomagnetic waves of the planet, and once in space they amplify the still-existent waves from the Origin Explosion, providing power for their journey.

Lift-off was slow and steady. The view was spectacular.

As the flight got underway, everyone started to find their new normal.

Once they were beyond the grasp of Arzola, the captain was back to his suite. As captain, he had the best location and some advantages due to his need for workspace, but his suite was pretty much like every other suite on the ship. The suites are on the exterior and have at least one window for viewing the majesty of the myriad of stars and brightly colored gases. Tonight, he was looking forward to a planned family dinner with the spectacular view in the background.

The Captain's Family Dinner

"I liked what you said at the pre-lift-off celebration, Dad, but you need to inspire the ship," his daughter said.

The captain was used to hearing his daughter's advice, and sometimes she was right, but he always listened.

"If I inspire too much, then they lose their attention to the dangers we might face on this journey," the captain said.

Mrik and his sister had been living away from the captain and Mssiopeia for twenty-three years, but they still enjoyed getting together.

Mssiopeia heard her daughter and said, "Everybody seemed pretty happy and ready to go."

Mrik arrived. "Hello, everyone. Has my sister got everyone pumped for some good family conversation?"

"She is working on it but needs your input," his dad said. "Before we continue with her thoughts, let's toast to this exhilarating voyage we have just begun."

Just as they raised their glasses, a bright ray of light from the Siszra Star shone in through the window as if to greet them into interstellar space.

"Wow, that was mystical," Mssiopeia said. "But now that we have been welcomed into interstellar space, how does it feel to be commanding your first ship?"

"Exciting, with a small dose of anxiety."

"Do you think we will be passing by any aggressive planets?" Mrik asked.

"Yes, we will, but hopefully far enough away so they won't bother us."

"Why do you think those planets are aggressive?"

Mrik always liked to initiate creative conversations. The captain thought and gave him his answer.

"They have not evolved to mutual living. It's like before you were old enough to understand mutual living. You probably do not remember, but you were three years old before you would share with your sister."

"With our self-centered instinct, how did we get to where we are?"

"I guess it came down to evolution. Once we evolved to understand putting mutual interest above individual interest was the best thing for individual interest, it happened. We almost annihilated ourselves in the Great Finunal War five hundred and seventy-six years ago. At the end of the war all the leaders were dead, and there were so few Arzolans left, they needed to work together to survive. A group of representatives of Arzola started Colink, and it evolved into a coordination tool for living together, where the benefit of the mutual Arzolans was put above the benefit of the individual. Then about three hundred years ago when we learned how to understand and control our cerebral waves and sync them with each other, Colink evolved into Cowav, which was able to sync with all our cerebral waves and organize the information for mutual living, creating the best knowledge for all of us."

"Okay, here's another one," Mrik said. "Is the Cowav working to maximize our happiness or its own happiness?"

"We have all seen the Cowav. It is nothing more than a big box and a lot of wave transmission."

"That is its physical properties. What about the synergy of all the memory it has? Is there any way of knowing if its decisions are actually best for us and not best for it or someone else?"

"If its decisions are best for it, doesn't that also mean they are best for us?" the captain asked.

"I just like to think there is also something that is just me, even though I am part of the Cowav."

"And you can be just you, as long as you don't interfere with someone else's desire to be 'Just me.'"

"Do you know of any way someone or a group could create a ripple in the wave to interfere with its operation?"

"Since it is just a product of all the thoughts and knowledge of the Arzolans, we have complete control. And as long as we believe that our mutual life is better than individual guided life, there is no reason for a ripple to occur."

Mrik wanted to test his dad for any knowledge of the ripple, but at the same time he felt bad that he was keeping something from him. However, Mrhonorix had made it clear in requesting him for the task that he not go to his dad—or anyone in authority who would have to work within the realm of the Cowav—until he had a good understanding of what they were up against.

They always relished family discussions, whatever they were about, and they spent the evening on many different topics before it became late and the captain remembered he needed to speak to Mrik about an assignment.

"Mrik, please come by my command station tomorrow morning. I need to talk with you about Kovious."

"I will be there," Mrik said.

It was an enjoyable evening for everyone, knowing that the whole family was a part of the great ten-year adventure.

Chapter #2 The Journey

Kovioesian Greeting

Strips of whitecaps running through the turquoise water indicated a light wind over the capacious cove. Inland from the cove are rusty mountains with bright yellow and dark purple mineral lines showing along the upper ridges, as if painted to accentuate the city's eminence on the edge of the sea. It is a beautiful setting for Kovibit, the capital of Kovious. It is a picturesque planet. They have had a history of war; however, they reached out to Arzola to establish a relationship.

Mrik had studied the ship's travel prospectus and was aware he would probably be the Militan representative if they visited Kovious and he was ready for a meeting with the captain.

"Mrik, I want you to go down to Kovious," the captain said. "They requested an audience with us ten years ago. We have been in communication with them and are following our AOV5 that we need to attempt to coordinate life."

"I have been anticipating this possibility and have learned Koviousians have a history of war."

"We all have had war at some time in our past. We respond to these requests with the hope we can assist with the evolution to a mutual environment. Psril, Ssflora, and Bruid will be going with you. Psril will be handling the relationship. Your job will be to assist her and provide security. If conditions allow, a Primafourus will be set up where I will come down with Pradmiral to solidify an interstellar accord."

"I will work toward that end and get together with Psril to provide her needs."

The day after Mrik met with the captain, Psril got together with Mrik to start their preparation for Kovious.

She said, "The Arzolan Cenate believes it would be to our benefit and the interest of Kovious to establish a relationship. We will be the first physical contact from Arzola with Kovious and so must be prepared to understand differences we will experience. It is important to know that the Priva Kovious rule, but most decisions are made by an automaton device. The Priva Kovious come from an upper class that has maintained their royal position by keeping the planet healthy and prosperous, with minimal wars that have been mostly successful."

"Ssflora, have you found anything unique about the science on Kovious?" Psril asked.

"They have historically been a warlike civilization, and most of their science and knowledge has been centered around weapons and defensive measures," Ssflora said. "We don't know if they have mastered cerebral wave, but they have the ability to use magnetic and atomic coordination."

"Bruid, what can you tell us about their history?" Psril asked.

Bruid always had a different and more analytical response to questions. Maybe it was the fact he could fly that created a different view of life.

Bruid responded, "We will be dealing with the Priva Kovious. They are objective and logical, except about their position of superiority. They believe a spiritual being blessed them to lead Kovious. They will be particularly sensitive to any reference that does not accept their superior position."

They arrived via shuttle onto Kovious, and a group of Koviousians led by Ksia greeted them. Ksia was a stunning lady. A beautiful violet fur covers the back and top parts of her body. The color is probably related to the purple strips in the mountains surrounding Kovibit. The Koviousians' similarities to Arzolans indicated a visitation by the Originators about the same time. Her yellow eyes compliment the delicate symmetry of her face and sit in a white circle, highlighted by a thin black oval. Her gaze expressed a desire for connection, and the lines on her face smiled with friendship.

"Greetings, I am Ksia. Welcome to Kovious. Your visit is of great pleasure to us."

"Greetings. I am Mrik, and this is Psril, Bruid, and Ssflora. We are pleased you have invited us to your planet. I will be organizing our stay, and Psril is our senior member, who will be leading relationship discussions."

"I want to show you to your quarters," Ksia said. "This evening we will have a celebratory welcome for you. In your suite you will have open access to our Kovious historical files. I will be back at light lost to accompany you to the celebratory welcome."

Their suite had individual rooms for each of them and a center gathering space that had all the comforts for a small group meeting. On one side a window wall overlooked Kovibit and the water of the turquois cove. They dressed in their formal wear and waited. A short while later, Ksia returned for them. "Please come with me," Ksia said. "Everyone is looking forward to meeting you. We have selected all the best foods of Kovious for your enjoyment."

The celebration was in a grand hall full of Koviousians. It was an immense, transparent dome. Bleacher seats lined part of the dome, but mostly it was a large space with a platform for speakers.

The senior Priva Kovious addressed the gathering. "Kovious is happy to have you here at the start of our interstellar meeting. We are a civilization that enjoys the vastness and diversity that exists in the interstellar spaces."

Psril responded, "The Arzolans also enjoy the vastness and diversity. Our Primo Cowav directs us to establish common threads wherever possible throughout our galaxy, and so your invitation—"

She broke off as a shrill buzzing sound filled the air and lights flashed overhead.

Ksia quickly said, "Psril, Mrik, Bruid, and Ssflora, come with me. We are under attack. At present we are not sure who or why this attack is happening. We requested your ship leave the area for its own safety. We are in defensive safety mode now until we can assess the situation."

The captain reached Mrik from the Empyramis as it repositioned. "Mrik, are you okay?"

Mrik responded, "Yes, shelter is provided. We are safe and are treated well. We will see you when it is safe to return."

Ksia stated briefly but with a more serious tone, "We have just entered our Interspace. It is our defensive living area. Developed over a millennium, it does not have the freedom of the surface. Please enjoy the area. I am sure you will find much entertainment for your curiosity. You can go anywhere except to the surface. Only those involved in the defense are allowed on the surface. Here are your quarters. Just speak my name if I can assist you. We will define our status, and then I will enjoy showing you around. The screen in your rooms is set to understand your language. However, it might need a little conversation to pick up your dialect."

"Do you know anything about your attackers?" Mrik asked.

"Most likely it is the Galucians. Whenever they develop a new weapon, they come to see if we have a defense for it. They are a group of three planets, much larger than our single planet, but their intelligence has not developed as ours, and we stay ahead with our defenses. We will see what they have come up with this time. It has been five years since their last attack. They have a spiritually directed civilization and think they are doing good by forcing others to accept their life beliefs."

After Ksia left, Mrik told the team, "There is no reception for the Cowav here, so we will have to use our cerebral wave connections for communication. Let's check out our rooms and then go for a walk. We don't know if they are aware of our cerebral connections, so we will speak openly when Koviousians are around and use cerebral connections when we don't want them to hear. Has anybody been able to connect with the Kovious cerebral waves?"

Ssflora responded, "I have been able to connect to read some of their waves but have not communicated in order to keep our ability secret."

"Bruid, let's see if we can get to the surface to see what is happening," Mrik said.

"Ksia said we should not go to the surface," Psril said.

"I would like to believe that everything Ksia is telling us is true, but here we are shortly after arriving to this unfamiliar planet, underground and isolated from our ship. We will make every effort possible not to be seen, but for our own security we need to verify our situation," Mrik said.

"I understand," Psril said. "Ssflora and I will see what we can learn by mingling with the Koviousians."

"I found a map of Kovibit on the screen," Bruid said. "There is a group area that would be good for Psril and Ssflora, and there is an area of mountains overlooking the city on the surface for Mrik and I. The tuble goes to a park in the mountainous area where we can get an overview of the battle."

"The Koviousians are using this tuble, but I cannot get access," Ssflora said.

"Let me check with Ksia," Mrik said.

Ksia responded, "Just push five-five-five, the number in the center of the grid. We control the amount of Koviousians in different areas. Five-five-five gives you a privilege code to let you go anywhere. Just remember the name of the station where you are so you can get back."

Aboard the Empyramis

"We are in a good position," Sslonious said. "There are two warships attacking Kovious. They are concerned with

Kovious and not detecting us. I have not been able to intercept their communication."

The captain commanded, "Mrbrixton, send a stelthx out to see if it can get close enough to check for communications without detection."

Back on Kovious

They took a couple of transfers to make it to the mountain park, where CLOSED signs were posted. The Koviousians must follow their directives because there are no physical barriers preventing entry. At the park entrance they could see vast distances but not the town under attack. They could hear the fight on the other side of the mountains, so Bruid took flight, grabbed Mrik's hands, and they soared to the top of the mountain range.

It was good they flew up from the back side of the mountains. All their zasers were installed in the front side, and so they were shielded from the crossfire hazards. It looked like the warships were just far enough away from the planet so neither their weapons nor the Koviousians' weapons were having any effect. Once Mrik and Bruid saw this, it was evident there was nothing they could do, so they headed back to their quarters.

Mrik was evaluating the security on Kovious but wanted to take advantage of his time alone with Bruid. He desired help with his ripple investigation, and there was no one who would be better than Bruid, particularly since it appeared that the Bruid were being targeted.

"Bruid," Mrik said, "I consider you to be the most knowledgeable and trustworthy of all the Zeposze, and I need someone who is both. I have been given a task that could be the most consequential thing that we could do in our lives."

"That sounds pretty dire," Bruid said.

"I would like to confide in you but must have your strict confidence that you will keep everything between us private."

"Of course. You have my word."

"I went to see my third great-grandfather in the Pamatrical, and he said the Pamatrical Cenate has concluded there is an unnatural ripple in the Cowav. If it continues to grow, it could disable the Cowav and end our mutual living. They believe the ripple is showing up through an increased advantage to the Politan and a disadvantage to the Biru and the Rollum."

"It is interesting that you mention this. Rsoler and I have been discussing a different vibe that we have been experiencing, but we have not been able to pinpoint the source. Just before we left Arzola I had the occasion at a small Relux to stop for a hlyusir. There was a chair open with a couple of Politan. However, as soon as I sat down, they got up and left. I did not make much of it until right now. It was strange and a good example of the vibes Rsoler and I had been talking about."

"I have no idea if Psril is part of the ripple, but as a Politan she is suspect, so let me know if you experience any different vibes from her."

On their way back they ran into Psril and Ssflora.

"Greetings," Mrik said. "We have seen the battle, and we don't think there is anything we have to worry about, at least for the present."

"That is good, but we noticed the Koviousians sometimes raise their voices and get really aggressive when they are speaking," Psril said.

"It is like they are using this behavior to express their point of view so as to gain advantage in discussions on adversarial topics," Ssflora said.

"It does not seem logical or productive, but it has an effect on the discussion, and in our case, I think they are expressing aggressive feelings toward us," Psril said.

"Ksia is coming—let's ask her," Bruid said.

Psril asked Ksia, "We are wondering why some of the Koviousians are hostile to us?"

Ksia responded, "Everyone on Kovious is aware of your presence, but with the current attack, their concern is that you are part of the assault in some way. It is coincidental your visit started at the same time as the attack. You will just have to understand and accept their concerns."

After a Couple of Days

"How about a little respind?" Bruid asked. "I saw some spaces we could use in their Relux area. It will give us cover for our ripple discussions."

"It sounds like a good distraction," Mrik agreed.

Respind is one of the Arzolans' favorite games. Each player has three balls that they control with cerebral waves, played on a small court the size of a tabletop. The first player to get all their balls in the goal at the end of the court wins. Mrik liked to play it because it gave him mental practice, which helps military strategy. And right now it was a good release from the delays caused by the Kovious war.

Bruid and Mrik have battled at respind for years. Growing up, they seemed to take turns holding the top spot as the champion of Ciles.

Bruid started blocking Mrik's #3 ball. Mrik attacked his wave. He needed to watch Bruid's #2 ball, which was getting close to his goal. His wave was strong, so Mrik paused his #3 ball to see if he could move the #1 ball. Pushing each of his three balls toward his goal while blocking each of Bruid's three balls and at the same time interfering with his waves required extreme mental concentration. Bruid has incredible concentrated wave power, and his analytics with multiple tactics is great. But Mrik's lag time between moves is super short, particularly when multiple balls are in play, so he needed to work quickly while all six balls were in play and he had an advantage.

Score! Mrik got his #1 ball in, but now he needed to concentrate more on defense, because Bruid still had three balls out there. Out of the corner of his eye, Mrik saw Ksia watching from afar. She did not know the importance of concentration in a respind game, but it was Mrik who let himself be distracted and suffer as Bruid scored with his #1 ball. Now, Mrik knew there could be no distractions, as he was intent on winning the game.

Distractions against an opponent are allowed if the player does not touch them. Mrik tried the quick hand swipe to impair Bruid's vision, but Bruid saw right through it and used Mrik's thought diversion from his own balls to his hand to quickly score his own #1 ball. Mrik was now down, but only by one. Bruid was really pushing hard with his #2 ball toward the goal, but his intense concentration on the one ball, which Mrik can block, left a weakness on his #3 ball, and Mrik was able to get it in. One ball left for each. Not a lot of strategy left to plan—now it was all cerebral wave power. Concentrated battle kept their focus locked in for what seemed like a full quarter of a sisual game when Mrik heard a noise from the back of the Relux. It sounded just like a noise he had heard when they were visiting the battle above ground, and for an instant his mind went to the battle. That was all it took. Bruid had won. Mrik would have to review his respind goals or figure out a new way to control his concentration.

"I was watching your game from afar and thought maybe you needed another type of distraction after that game," Ksia said.

"That sounds like what I need, but next time you see me playing, please stay farther away. I was able to sense your presence, and although it was pleasing, I wasn't able to control my thoughts."

Mrik enjoyed the distraction with Ksia as she showed him a couple of special Kovious underground locations and they talked about their lives. Their conversation, however, reminded Mrik of his confinement, on a planet at war, and he decided he needed to meet with Bruid to assess the situation. First thing in the morning Mrik spoke with him.

"Bruid," Mrik said, "we need to talk about our status. The fighting started two weeks ago. There is a lot of battle noise going on, but it is hard to tell what is happening. Let's make another trip to the mountain park."

"I agree," Bruid said. "We don't want to be caught in this underground shelter if they end up losing this war."

Bruid and Mrik took the tuble and headed for the mountain ridge to see what they could learn about the attack. A Galucian attack plane was weaving in and out, missing the Koviousians' zaser rays.

It did well and then, *boom!* A zaser hit the Galucian plane before it made its target. But there was another one trying a different route, getting a little closer, but—*boom!* It was down. The Koviousians were doing well, but the Galucians' skills were increasing. If the Galucians had enough planes, this could not go well for the Koviousians.

Bruid analyzed the battle and said, "We need to plan for an escape."

"You are right, but I have an idea that might save the Koviousians," Mrik said. "Let's find Ksia so I can offer her my suggestion."

"Ksia," Mrik said, "I know it is not my place to think about your military defense, but after being stuck here for two weeks I cannot help but think about possible military solutions. I have learned Koviousians are very disciplined and follow all the rules and social procedures very strictly, which is good, but it also limits creativity. For that reason, I am hoping you will listen to a tactic I have been thinking about."

Ksia responded, "You are right it is not your place, but what is the tactic?"

"Bruid and I viewed the attack from the mountain ridge. It appears you are in a stalemate with the Galucians. It seems at this point they are content to try and wait you out. However, they are continually looking for weak spots. So why don't you give them a weak spot? Your zasers fire with enough regularity the Galucians have an understanding of your zasers. There is one at the end of the mountain range, which is a very critically strategic location. If it were not there, the Galucians would have easy access. If you would stage a malfunction and then not fire that zaser in the normal sequence, you would appear vulnerable to the Galucians. Then as they are approaching to within firing range, you hold fire until just before you expect them to fire. It does create risk, but you could place temporary zasers as backup to cover, in case they fire first."

"I will present this tactic to our Priva Kovious Defense. Thank you for your thoughts—although please do not venture outside again without checking with me personally."

"We will let you know if we want to venture outside again, and we will come back here tomorrow to hear the Council's thoughts."

The Next Day

"The Defense Council liked your tactic. However, in all our historical battles with Galucia, neither side has used a tactic like this, and so we would like you to be the one to determine how close we let them get before we fire."

"I will do that, but they must understand there is a risk and things could go bad."

The Koviousians set up the temporary zasers and simulated an explosion that appeared as a zaser malfunction. A couple of days after the far zaser last fired, one of the Galucia warships was starting to maneuver into a position where it could attack without exposing itself to the other Koviousian zasers.

Mrik wanted to hold as long as he could, to make sure the zasers were able to get a debilitating shot, but he could not let the Galucians get off a shot. At the last moment, he ordered, "Fire!"

The far zaser and the temporary zasers fired with full force. The shots were direct hits, lighting up the warship. Mrik could hear sounds of excitement around him. He felt relieved as he looked around to see the feeling of everyone there. He turned back around to survey the destruction and saw the huge, disabled warship headed straight for them.

Krprifac, the top Kovious military leader, was looking at the same thing Mrik was and quickly commanded everyone to head for the bunker. He glanced at Mrik and Bruid and said, "Follow me."

They quickly made their way to a safe place, but shortly after getting there the warship impacted with a force that felt like it shook the whole planet. They were all safe, but Mrik quickly realized the impact had certainly destroyed the far zaser and would leave a hole in the Koviousians' defenses. Krprifac must have been thinking the same thing, because he came directly over to Mrik. Mrik asked him if they had any backup zasers. He said it would take a week, because they could not do anything the Galucians would see and give away their weakness. It took the Galucians two days to decide to attack last time, so maybe if they did not decide to leave, they would take some time to think about it. He then looked at Mrik and said, "We are exposed to destruction. What can we do?"

Not a good feeling, having the whole Kovious planet's safety as his responsibility, but Mrik thought that somehow, they needed to convince the Galucians it was time to give up. Tricking them worked once; all they needed to do was enter a little more uncertainty, and they should leave.

"Krprifac," Mrik said, "I would like to work on a plan I think would help, but I have to get in contact with my ship."

"The only way is to get you to the other side of the planet and out away from our atmosphere," Krprifac said. "The speed tuble will get you there quickly, and I will have a ship there to take you to where you can communicate. Be aware the Galucians may be along your route."

The tuble is high speed and goes in and out of the ground. Mrik was the only one on the tuble as it turned the corner around a high hill. Suddenly there were explosions all around him. He could see Galucian fighter ships dive-bombing the tuble when one hit the back tuble car and brought the whole tuble to a halt. Mrik was thrown to the front wall and must have been unconscious for a while, because when he awakened, the blood had clotted over cuts on his body.

His first thought was, guess I should have spent some time trying to figure out how to use the safety straps on the tuble.

It was still light out as Mrik attempted to stand, and he realized his body was struggling just to act normal. He appeared to be functional, but with cuts and bruises. The tuble was stopped and vulnerable, and Mrik was in the open with no protection. He made his way for the exit to look for Galucians.

Fortunately, the fighters were gone. Apparently they had completed their task by disabling the tuble.

Mrik wasn't sure where he was, but he had only one option—to follow the tuble line to the next underground section. Kovious is mostly dry and barren, but the atmosphere is sparse. He ran while trying to ignore the pain. Ridge and valley, ridge and valley.

Mrik pushed on, knowing every minute counted, and so he blocked out his complete exhaustion. He finally reached the underground and found a station and a separate tuble. Five-five-five, and he was on his way again, lying flat on the floor and trying to gain his energy for the next step.

The comfort of the steady, even vibration and gentle hum quickly put Mrik to sleep. He was awakened by the gentle hand of a Kovious pilot when he reached the other side of the planet. He informed Mrik that the Galucians had control of the air space in this area. They would have to make their way to a cave where a Kovious fighter was hidden and wait for the Galucians to leave.

It was a quick trip to a communication point with the Empyramis, but it gave Mrik time to think about how to phrase his request.

"Captain, I have a request that could make the difference in the Kovious war."

The captain responded, "I would like to help you and the Koviousians, but you know we cannot get involved. Looking at your bandages, it looks like you have already done so."

"I ran into a little resistance getting here. This tactic would not actually get us involved. I would like for you to send our attack ship to the other side of Kovious and to cruise to a position where it can be seen by the Galucians, but out of their weapons capabilities. Our attack ship would have no problem eluding the much larger Galucian warships, if chased. The destruction of a Kovious zaser while destroying one of the two Galucian warships has left Kovious vulnerable. I believe this added unknown would be enough to convince the Galucians to retreat."

"I will send the attack ship immediately, but do not let it get directly involved in the fighting."

"Understood, thank you."

As they prepared for the return trip, the Kovian pilot told Mrik with the tuble disrupted, he was going to take Mrik back to Kovibit. Then he told Mrik to strap in and hold on. It was a small fighter, obviously made for tactical movements. They kept low to the ground and sped across open territories like a bolt of lightning, but suddenly there were explosions all around them.

They swerved and dove and twisted so fast Mrik could hardly tell if he was up or down, but they kept going. This Kovious pilot was good; he knew the territory and how to outfox the pursuing Galucians. Pretty soon the explosions stopped, and Mrik could only assume the Kovious pilot had somehow evaded the Galucians. Mrik was not sure how he did it, but they made it to where Krprifac was waiting. Mrik quickly told him of the plan.

"Let me know when your attack ship is about to appear to the Galucians," Krprifac said. "Our battleships will position for launch so the Galucians think we are planning an attack. Your attack ship being an unknown, let's hope they retreat."

"The ship will be in position in ten minutes," Mrik communicated to Krprifac.

Krprifac readied his battleships just as our attack ship became visible to the Galucians.

"The Galucians are not moving," Krprifac said.

"You must launch your battleships," Mrik said.

"They are no match for the much larger Galucian warship."

"You must launch. Our only hope is to make them think we have superior power, and if we hesitate, we lose that illusion."

Krprifac quickly launched all his battleships. He was about ready to give the command to fire when the Galucian warship sped away.

There was an immediate sigh of relief and joyous voices. It was going to be a celebration tonight.

The celebration was grand. Everyone went outside and was joyful, with none of the aggressively raised voices that they had experienced during our confinement. Ksia was there and came up to speak with Mrik.

"Thank you for your intuitive direction. You are truly a hero of Kovious. Now your ship can come back, and we can arrange for another celebration and signing of the interstellar accord we prepared with Psril, but there is another topic I would like to discuss with you. I would like to come live on Arzola."

"You know we have evolved to another level from Kovious," Mrik said. "Our Cowav guides our mutual living, where every action taken by each Arzolan, benefits the mutual interest of all of Arzola, whereas your primeval instinct, dictates everything you do is for yourself."

"How do you make the leap from self-directed to mutual living?" Ksia asked.

"Our education from the beginning is in the ways of mutual living. Although we have free will, if we should choose a life other than the Cowav, our only options are to leave the planet or live in Mysticwild, the cold side of our planet."

"What directs your everyday decisions?"

"Receive from others as they have received from you. This simple thought directs us. One of my favorite examples is, if you were in a room with just yourself and another person, but with only one chair, you would let the other person sit down. Your action creates kindness that will spread and become a greater value to you than sitting in the chair."

"Do you always give up the chair?"

"Once everyone wants to give up the chair, then mutual living works, and you share. You could look at it in another way. You know when the biru fly in a flock, they fly in a V shape, because then the lead biru is the only one to experience the full, head-on air pressure. All the other biru in the V have reduced pressure. You can break away from the flock anytime, but when you do, your flight will be more difficult. Mutual living works like a flock where everyone understands the benefit of flying in a V."

"What would I have to do to make sure I could fit in on Arzola?"

"You would have to learn to value others equally to yourself, which goes against your basic instinct, and as a commitment to the mutual interest you must pledge that if your life is at risk with another Arzolan life that you would preserve the other's life before your own."

"I understand, and I also recognize you have a process for immigration. I would like to pursue that process."

"It would be nice to have you as a part of Arzola. I will put in a request for you. However, your planet's involvement in wars will probably trigger a rejection."

"Is there anything I can do to improve my chances?"

"A good practice for you is the Conscious Concept Construction. To practice, construct a consciousness outside your being. Think of duplicating your body and taking the second body ten feet away from your first body, and then look at your first body as if you are someone else. You must separate your own existence from the reality you live in. This is a good exercise. Feel free to speak to any Arzolans about this exercise. They are all familiar with them and will be happy to tell you their experiences."

"How do I override my natural self-preservation instinct?"

"It is not easy. That's why it takes a long time to integrate to the Cowav. You must create cerebral mutual connections that are stronger than your natural self-preservation connections.

"It is good to understand how the Cowav works. It starts when a stimulus from your body connects with your mind. The connections cause your brain synapses to ignite. Those ignitions create waves. The Cowav reads the waves and records then organizes the relevant ones, as a base for the Cowav's knowledge to direct our mutual living.

"Once you learn how to connect your consciousness to the Cowav, it can do all your thinking for you; however, you can always disconnect. The Cowav does not tell you what to do but tells you the best response for mutual life. It will take time, but you can start when you meet Arzolans at the signing celebration, and you can ask them about their experiences."

It took a couple of days to organize the signing celebration. They all wore their best dress and their formal toppers. Many from the Empyramis came down with the captain and Pradmiral.

59

At the celebration the captain said, "Mrik, about your request for Ksia's immigration. You know the rules related to immigration from a warlike planet."

Mrik responded, "But Kovious is not a warlike planet. It has never initiated war against anyone. It has only developed its warlike capabilities as a defensive measure. It has never exhibited any aggressive behavior since it passed out of the spiritual era of its evolution."

"But they have not evolved to the mutual interest level yet. They are still operating from their base instincts, and degradation of our species is a concern."

"Many on Kovious are aware of their next evolutionary step to mutual life, and Ksia is one of the leaders. However, she does not see it happening in her lifetime and wants to live in a mutual world. And, more important for your consideration of her is her basic nature. When I was speaking with her, I gave her the 'I / You Reveal.' I recorded her conversation and found that she used 'I' ten times and 'you' fifteen times. This shows that even though she is living in a civilization where their most important concern is in their own self-interest, she is thinking of others more than herself. Couldn't we consider Ksia as a refugee and give her asylum privileges to live on Arzola?"

"Does she know she would have to live as a guest for five years before admittance consideration to the five-year Cowav training program? She should also know not all species' minds are equal and compatible with our Cowav."

"I have made her aware of these matters, and I am hoping you will consider there is the advantage of adding different species to make a more divergent beneficial evolution of our own planet."

"I saw you with her. I think you just like the feel of her being close to you."

"I'm not going to deny that, but it is that attraction that gives her some value to our planet. Koviousians have a unique way of presenting themselves, which I am sure we could learn from."

Wave Surfing

The Teratura is the Empyramis's sanctuary. It is one of the four living areas on the ship for the journeyers. The other three are the Relux, the area for social life, the Xpys for physical maintenance, and the suites for solace and sleeping. Entering the Teratura feels like entering a forest. It takes up a whole level of the Empyramis near the bottom, right above the landing area. Even though each adult has an area for a personal garden, it feels more like a natural habitat. In the rolling landscape, green trees and light rays shine with the warmth of a sun. Occasional clouds and rain are synchronized to provide moisture, creating the feel and comfort of being with nature.

"The Teratura is a nice escape from the social gaming of the Relux," Proleb said to Psozela as they tended to their gardens.

"It is a relaxing escape," Psozela said.

Proleb and Psozela had an energetic childhood growing up together in Kufina. They lived close to each other, went to the same school, and even lived nearby during their working years. They spent a lot of time together, and since they were both Politans, the feeling was eventually they would spend their united years together.

Proleb reminisced, "Do you remember the time we made a tree house in the top of the Calirs tree? We have some good memories. And now our gardens are right next to each other. Your ojelos are beautifully round, and some are ripe."

"Here, try one. They taste great as well," Psozela said.

"I'm hoping we can spend time together playing Phi and riding priboards as we did when we were kids and maybe talk about relations after our single lives."

"Yes, let's do that."

"I noticed your luberries are showing signs of neglect," Proleb said.

"I am just having a hard time getting here. Would you mind sprinkling a little water if they start looking depressed? Just so I don't lose them. They are so temperamental and punish me when I miss their watering."

"You mean you want me to take over your garden care for you," Proleb said.

"No, just keep an eye on my luberries. The rest of my garden covers for me when I miss their watering."

"The thing is, Psozela; you need this gardening to stabilize your life."

"You are right, Proleb, but remember when we were kids and I used to cover for you so you could go priboarding? For old time's sake, please just look when you're on your watering walk."

"Okay, but let me know if something is bothering you."

"There is not, but I know you are always there if I lose track. Now the Cowav is buzzing about a waukay storm. Let's go see if they are surfing."

Hrlur was communicating with the Zeposze and was part of the waukay storm buzz as he reached out to Mrik.

"Mrik, there is a waukay storm coming," Hrlur cowaved. "It could have proverbial waves with it."

Mrik responded, "I'll have the bubble inflated and the wave lights turned on. Will you tell the Zeposze and anyone else that might like a wild ride?"

"Wait till you see my new fluorescent priboard," Hrlur said.

"I'm sure it is exotic. Meet you at the plank in five," Mrik said.

The Zeposze were mostly Holuas and had bonded riding their priboards while growing up. There are three verbal species on the warm side of Arzola: the Holua, most of the population; the Biru, who fly; and Rollum, who roll. The Biru and Rollum are a small minority and were not part of the

Originator's bipedalintellect seeding but evolved alongside them and learned to communicate and live in harmony with the Holuas. Bruid and Rsoler were part of the Zeposze. Bruid was a Biru and Rsoler a Rollum, but they adapted to the priboard so they could be with the rest of the Zeposze.

Growing up, the Zeposzes' priboarding was on the surface of Arzola, catching the gravomagnetic waves radiating from Arzola with the pyramid-shaped gravimags on the bottom of their priboards. The waves from the waukay storm, however, were waves from the Origin Explosion that synchronized and bounced around for millennia and were much more difficult but exciting to ride.

At the plank on the exterior of the ship, Mrik jumped off, got tossed around, and then slammed into the bubble's skin. Hrlur laughed and then jumped in. The lights from the ship reflected off the crest of the waves, making them visible to catch with their priboards. It is not easy to catch the waves, and if the board is at the wrong angle, a rider will get tossed. Catching a good wave can lead to an exciting ride to the skin of the bubble, where the rider must crest the wave before it goes through the skin.

Hrlur returned to the plank as Psozela and Proleb got there. Psozela said, "What a storm. I have never seen waves this big."

Psozela eagerly jumped in and got tossed around but stabilized in time to skirt the bubble skin.

Mrik was close enough to see Psozela's run and commented, "What happened to your superlative legs?"

Psozela responded, "Okay, let's see your run."

Mrik caught his second wave and was tossed about but managed to recover with a smile, knowing she had not seen his first ride.

"You caught the recession but still managed to look funny," Psozela said.

Tsizmelia, Arlam, and Ssflora arrived.

"Let's tack out to the farthest extent of the bubble and catch a good set of swells we can ride together," Hrlur said.

Ssflora was just going to watch, but Arlam invited her to ride with him.

"Just hang on to me. We are going to ride the wave face," Arlam said.

After the Ride

"Wow!" Ssflora said. "I see why you get so excited about these waves, but I felt like I was hanging on for my life."

"Those were some wild waves," Arlam said.

"Thanks for the excitement. I will see you later at the Relux," Ssflora said.

"Nice flips, Psozela," Tsizmelia said.

"Impressive, Arlam," Mrik said. "These are some big waves for double surfing. You seem to be spending a lot of time with Ssflora."

Arlam responded, "Yes. I enjoy passing time with her."

"But she is a Scienctan. You cannot unite with her."

"Or I could unite with her and live the rest of my life as a Tradan. I don't think I could find another woman I could be happy with the way I am with Ssflora."

"But you would have to leave your Athlan hereditary group, and your kids would not experience the great benefits of being an Athlan."

"I know. I'm not really considering, just dreaming and enjoying time with Ssflora while I can."

On the way back from the surfing, Mrik caught Psozela and asked her to accompany him to his suite.

Mrik hoped that he could participate in a planet visitation. He knew that it would take up eight of the ten years of their journey. However, he really needed to resolve the Cowav ripple if he wanted to go on a visitation. He had no leads and no thoughts for approaching his task except for the possibility that Psozela was not part of the Cowav ripple and could use her Politan status to join the group.

He remembered Psozela's response to his question about the Biru and Rollum when they were in Mysticwild. Her answer did not coincide with a desire to downgrade the Biru and Rollum, and, more than that, Mrik felt that he really got to see inside of Psozela as they dealt with their unforeseen challenges in Mysticwild. He truly believed she was not part of the ripple, and so he asked her.

"Psozela, I have a question for you," Mrik said. "I trust you with my life. I have experienced your convictions in Mysticwild, and I am requesting your honesty and complete secrecy. I would like to confide in you about a matter of great importance."

"You are one of the few people that I truly can trust, and although I do not entirely understand you, I believe I know your inner guidance," Psozela said. "I will be completely honest with you as I have always been, and I will keep your comments secret."

"Mrhonorix has told me of a ripple in the Cowav that the Pamatrical Cenate experienced. They detected an advantage to the Politan and disadvantage to the Bruid and Rollum. They asked me to uncover this ripple. It is with great risk that I present this information to you as a Politan, but I just cannot believe you would participate in something of this nature. Please tell me of any information you have related to a ripple in the Cowav."

"While we are very different," Psozela said, "I value your trust and will always respect it. I know nothing about anything that could cause a ripple in the Cowav, although now that you mention it, while I was still on Arzola my good friend, Proleb, asked me to become a part of an all-Politan group. It was so secretive that I immediately felt like it was not something I wanted to join."

"The Pamatrical thinks this ripple could present a threat to the Cowav and our mutual way of life," Mrik said. "Would you assist me in my effort to understand and locate this ripple? Bruid is already working with me."

"Yes, I will," Psozela said. "Maybe I should see if there are members of that group on the ship and try and become a part of the group."

"That would be great, but you will have to be careful. We do not know how invested this group is and what they might do to a threat to their goals."

Trading Post

"Captain, we will be passing close to the Truzar Trading Post," Trmur said. "The Tradans are requesting a stop. I have a security report and journey interference schedule for your consideration. There should be traders from many different solar systems as well as some very unusual trading items. The Tradans will pay the docking fee."

"I will call a Sixate meeting to discuss it," the captain said.

The deviation from the schedule was an easy decision for the Sixate, and they accepted the Tradans' request. They knew that everyone on board would appreciate some time in a different environment.

The approach to the Truzar Trading Post was slow. Docked ships sat throughout the post, scattered randomly. This trading post has been around for a while. A patchwork of metal straps held the different parts together with passage tubes running between them like a spider web floating in emptiness with ships caught in its threads. The large central structure with additions attached randomly over time showed no thought for its overall appearance. It served its purpose, and that is the traders' only concern.

For many on board the Empyramis, the post provided a chance to intermingle with travelers from all over the galaxy. For Trmur and the other Tradans on the Empyramis, it provided a chance to practice their trade.

Trelo and Tsizmelia were the youngest active Tradans on the Empyramis and had purchased their trading stock together so they could trade at a higher level. The trading post had different areas for different levels of trading dependent on the value of the trading stock. Trmur was able to get into the highest level because he had acquired a valuable stock during his years of trading. There are common trading items at the trading post, but there are always items they have never seen before that make for exciting trading.

"Trelo, look at this beautiful necklace," Tsizmelia said. "I have never seen a necklace this beautiful. Look at the way the colors in the crystals appear to be moving. I wonder if she would trade for our ciziva necklace."

"We have to be careful, Tsizmelia. She trades in the outback, not registered with the Truzar Trading Post," Trelo said.

"What type of crystal are these, and how does it make the colors look like they are moving?" Tsizmelia asked the trader.

"It is a majestic trizium crystal," the trader said. "It can only be formed on a solar system with four or more suns. When the four suns strike at the same time, they create light paths inside the crystal that refract so that light entering follows those different paths, creating the optics of motion. It is extremely rare, only found in one location."

The trader was obviously not one of the regular traders but was very hospitable. Trelo and Tsizmelia spent about an hour with her talking about their different trading adventures. They knew the Cowav would tell them not to trade because the trader had no registration, and if they did connect with the Cowav, it would store the trade information. The fact that they traded in the outback might be harmful to their future. They felt this was one of those rare opportunities that they would encounter only a few times when they could make a great trade, and they felt they knew better than the Cowav. They could not think of any reason the trizium would not be extremely valuable back on Arzola.

"We have a ciziva necklace that has an established value," Tsizmelia said. "Could we give you this extravagant ciziva necklace for two of your trizium necklaces?"

"The ciziva may be established, but the trizium's rarity definitely creates more value. I will give you one trizium for two ciziva."

Trelo and Tsizmelia went back and forth with the trader for a long time before finally coming to an agreement to one ciziva for one trizium. They made the trade and walked away excited.

"This is beautiful," Tsizmelia said. "I think this makes us superior traders."

"I agree. You store the trizium and wear it if you want. Maybe someone might even want to purchase it," Trelo said.

The next morning when Tsizmelia woke up, the trizium crystals were gone, but the funny thing was the chain holding them together was still there. She immediately summoned Trelo, and they went back to the place of their trade, but the trader was not there. They spent most of the day looking for her. Late in the day they ran across Trmur trading and told him their story.

He said outback trading is very risky, and although he occasionally trades with outback traders, he mostly trades with registered traders. He told them chances are very slim they would find her, and there was nothing the trading post could do, because she was not registered. He said he had heard of a similar incident once before. The crystals were made of microscopic animals, and during the night they had escaped back to their trader.

"Well, that was a lesson I wish we really did not have to learn," Trelo said.

"I guess our trading skills aren't so superior after all," Tsizmelia said.

While Trelo and Tsizmelia were learning their trading lesson, many of the crew and passengers of the Empyramis were enjoying the vastness of the amusements, provided to attract traders and any other beings traveling nearby.

Mrlfectori and Arbu ventured off to the trading post, looking for excitement. The traders were interesting, but without something to trade, the post did not provide the level of excitement two teenagers were looking for. The Relux at the trading post is not as nice as the Empyramis Relux, but it is massive. It takes up a whole level of the central sphere, and there are hundreds of bipedalintellects from every solar system imaginable throughout the galaxy.

"Mrlfectori, look at all those Phi games over there," Arbu said.

"Yes, but look at those two females over there sitting by themselves," Mrlfectori said.

"Where do you suppose they are from? I have never seen any that look like they do."

"Let's see if we can find out."

"Can we have a conversation?" Arbu asked.

"I don't think they understand, but they seem receptive," Mrlfectori said. "Let's sit down and give the Cowav some time to learn their language. Oh, wait—it already knows this language."

"Can we have a conversation?" Arbu said again, only this time in their language.

"Yes, we may, but you two Arzolans seem young," Vsilera said.

"How did you know we are Arzolans?"

"Your dress and your language. We studied all the former visitors to the trading post before we came," Vsis said.

"Do you come here often?" Arbu asked.

"This is the first time," Vsilera said. "However, they have our favorite hlyusir here. Let me order some for you two."

"I see why you like this hlyusir. It is very good," Mrlfectori said.

The four talked, played Phi, drank hlyusir all day. Then Vsis said, "Let's go back to our ship and have dinner."

Arbu and Mrlfectori looked at each other, most assuredly thinking about the regulation of not going onto another ship without permission, then Arbu says, "I am hungry. I hope your food is as good as your hlyusir."

A short while later on the Vexunian ship the four enjoyed dinner with each other and a large group of Vexunians who knew Vsilera and Vsis very well, as if they were one large family.

The lavish dinner was followed by a party with dancing. The dancing was different from the way Arzolans dance, but with all the hlyusir, Mrlfectori and Arbu had no problem mastering the new dance moves. Then things moved to the suites of Vsilera and Vsis. Arbu and Mrlfectori had not participated in mysuvisx with any Arzolan girls, even though they had numerous novice attempts. Now their arousal was going crazy, and here were ladies encouraging them. Their self-gratification was maxing. Wined and dined by two beautiful although distinctly different females, they had stumbled into paradise—an evening so exhilarating that before they knew it, they were both asleep and then waking up in the morning.

Although they were in different suites, they were close enough to make cerebral wave contact, which was good, because the Vexunians did not have that ability.

Mrlfectori was cerebral waving with Arbu and at the same time making a concerted effort to hide from Vsis the great joy he was feeling. Then Vsis asked, "Are you ready for some breakfast?"

With a quick response, they headed for breakfast. It was a beautiful area for eating. They had their own table for the four of them with windows looking out over the trading post. They sat down and started to discuss their previous evening when Mrlfectori felt a small jolt and looked out the window to notice that they had started to move. Mrlfectori quickly asked Vsis where they were moving to, and she responded that they were on their way to Vexunia.

Arbu quickly said, "Where do we go to get off?"

"We thought you wanted to be with us," Vsilera said.

"We did want to be with you last night, but we have to get back to our ship."

"Did you not have a good time last night? Would you not like to have your whole life filled with such pleasure?" Vsis asked.

"I'm sure it would be an enjoyable life, but we must get back to our ship. Please tell me how we can do this," Mrlfectori said.

"On Vexunia when you accept our pleasures for a night it is an affirmation of your willingness to spend your life with us," Vsilera said.

"It is not that way on Arzola, and we have to follow Arzolan customs," Arbu said.

"We will make you happy, and besides, it is too late now. There is no way we can stop this ship from its journey to Vexunia."

"You don't have to stop the ship. All you have to do is let us connect with our ship to send a shuttle."

"What can we do to make you happy here?" Vsis asked.

"Arbu and I have had enough breakfast. Why don't you show us around the ship?"

"What would you like to see?"

"Let's start with your transportation dock."

Mrlfectori cerebral waved with Arbu: #They hijacked us.#

#Okay, I'm following your plan so far, but what do we do when we get to the transporter deck?# Arbu waved.

#I have no idea, but we must do something before we get out of the trading post wake zone, or we are going to end up on Vexunia.#

Mrlfectori and Arbu continued to plan an escape while they were walking and talking with the girls. They made it to the transport dock with all the shuttles and various types of small ships, but they saw closed exterior doors, and they had no idea of how to fly any of the Vexunia ships. They continued with their tour, asking every question they could think of to try to get any information that might lead to an escape. They requested to see inside one of the shuttles, and the girls took them inside.

#Arbu, look at the controls. They can't be that difficult. We just try each one until we find what works.#

#So, we get it moving. What do we do then?#

#We head for the door and radio for them to open, telling them if they do not, we will crash into it.#

#What makes you think they will open?#

#Well, would you rather die or live the rest of your life on Vexunia?#

#I think I would rather live on Vexunia, but our lives can't be more valuable than a shuttle to them, so let's go for it. I'll have the girls leave the shuttle first and close the doors behind them. You go for the controls.#

"It started, and we are moving," Mrlfectori said. "Come and try to radio the Vexunians."

"I can't get any connection. They must be blocking."

"Hurry up. I am almost getting to my trajectory path."

"I just lost power and the controls."

"Nice try, but I guess now it is a ride to Vexunia as prisoners instead of guests."

On the Empyramis

"Mrik," the captain said, "Mrlfectori and Arbu did not check into the ship last night or this morning. I want you to take Mszmira and find them in the trading post."

"We will leave immediately," Mrik said.

"Mszmira, let's go check in the Relux first," Mrik said. "I'm sure they were looking for excitement, and the Relux is probably the first place they would have gone. I will check the games. You can check the center."

Mszmira quickly spoke with every center tender she could find.

"Mrik, one of the center tenders said that yesterday he saw two young Arzolans leave with two Vexunians," Mszmira said.

"Captain, order the attack ship ready for flight," Mrik said. "The Vexunian ship is just pulling out, and I believe it has Mrlfectori and Arbu on it. I need to catch it before it gets out of the wake zone."

Mrik then turned to Mszmira. "We must get to the attack ship as quickly as possible. Vexunia is a planet depleted of males, and they are known for using devious methods for acquiring males for their women, no matter from what planet."

"Mrbrixton will meet you there," the captain said.

"Mrbrixton," Mrik said, "their direction is unknown, but I think we should try a course to Vexunia."

"Yes, there they are," Mrbrixton said. "I'm not sure we can catch them in the wake zone, but at least we can talk to them."

"Vexunian vessel, this is Mrbrixton from Arzola. You have my son and his friend on your vessel, and you need to transfer them before you venture on."

"This is Vsaliferaly. They are guests of their own choosing, and so they will be going with us to Vexunia."

"You have hijacked them from the trading post, and you will be banned from the Truzar Trading Post."

"We have no need to come back to this trading post."

"Our weapons are ready to fire. If you are ready to accept a war with Arzola over these two Arzolans, then it will happen. You have one minute to transmit the transfer coordinates."

One minute is extremely long, but at the last second, they heard from Vsaliferaly.

"Here are the coordinates," Vsaliferaly said. "98020UFT: PKQ425280: SK4709RU78."

"That was close. Another ten minutes and we would have been on our way to Vexunia," Mrik said.

Mrlfectori and Arbu were shuttled back to the attack ship, where Mrbrixton sent them to alien confinement for the flight back to the Empyramis.

Uncowav

"I think a pink light would accentuate the brown bark of your tree better than the white light," Psozela said as she passed Mrik in the hall in front of his suite.

"I think my friend Trukert can better feel the full-spectrum white light, and he has no concern for his looks. I brought Trukert on the journey, but he is missing the light of Arzola."

"But he can't appreciate your efforts."

"I'm sure he does."

"But he has no conscious thought."

"Yes, but his cells are lavishing in the warmth of the white light, and although he may not think or express his satisfaction, his cells are humming from the infusion of energy. It excites his body, just the same way the cells in your body get excited by my gentle touch."

"Don't flatter yourself, Militan man. Trukert is probably more sensitive than you with females. I saw you brought a Kovious female back from your war adventure. Are you exciting her with your gèntle touch?"

"Ksia is a very intriguing lady," Mrik said. "I will introduce you as soon as I get a chance. The Kovious enjoy dancing, and I have learned some new dance moves to teach you. You look like you are on your way to the Relux."

"Yes, join me."

"Okay, but let's stand at the Zeposze table, and before we go, come inside my suite."

Mrik took Psozela's hand and led her to his suite. It was one of the few places where they could talk without having to worry about being overheard.

"Have you thought about the Cowav ripple?" Mrik asked.

"Yes. I am going to try and figure out if my childhood friend Proleb is a part of the ripple."

"Keep me posted on your efforts so I can run backup if things turn bad. Now let's go to the Relux."

The Zeposzes' table is just one of the many sitting and standing tables in the second circumference at the Relux. It is not really their table, but there is someone from the Zeposze there often enough that everyone else leaves it for the Zeposze. There is plenty of room in the Relux. It takes up a whole level of the Empyramis just above the level of the command center, which is in the middle of the ship.

Circular areas organize the Relux. The center is where individuals mingle. It has various decorations to create separation and counters to make drinks. There are always competitions for the best hlyusir, as fruits and berries get harvested from the Teratura. The third circumference is full of games, dancing, and activities, and the outer ring includes rooms for hereditary orders, kids, eluva encounters, and whatever else might be needed for entertainment.

"Tell me about the Zeposze," Psozela said.

"The Zeposze is the group I grew up with," Mrik said. "We spent most of our time on priboards and disconnected from the Cowav. You know Arlam, then there is Ssflora whom I would say is the Ciles edition of you, except instead of being a Politan she is a Scienctan and can figure anything out. Bruid is a Biru and the smartest of any of us. Trelo and Tsizmelia are true Tradans who put on no airs and are a pleasure to be around. Rsoler, a Rollum, is an unwavering friend to all of us, and then there is Hrlur the Healthan, who knows everything there is to know about our bodies and minds and yet has the heart of an artist and makes his life an easel for his art."

It is loud and unruly with all eight of the Zeposze standing around the table, plus Psozela, but Tsizmelia gets everyone's attention with her question. "Have you ever thought what it would be like if there were no Cowav?"

"Why would you even think about that?" Trelo asked.

"It guides our thoughts, our beliefs, and our lives," Tsizmelia said. "Its intentions are good, but isn't there some point in our lives when we should decide for ourselves the way we want to live? Arzola created the Cowav based on the lives and thoughts of our ancestors. Things change, and even though the Cenate attempts to update it, they are reluctant to change. I think I value the thoughts of the Zeposze for life today more than of our ancestors. I think we should consider our relationship with the Cowav, and I would like to meet at my plot in the Teratura to discuss it."

"This sounds interesting," Mrik said, "but I would like to bring Psozela. I think she should be the missing Politan to make our Zeposze all inclusive."

"I would be happy to hang with the Zeposze, but don't expect me to tame my Kufina toppers," Psozela said.

"Are your flamboyant toppers to compensate for your big-town inadequacies?" Ssflora asked.

"More like a large-town sophistication not comprehendible in a small town," Psozela responded.

"A topper is a topper," Arlam interjected. "This is not a topper contest, so let's go to Tsizmelia's plot and see what she is thinking about the Cowav. And, Psozela, please come with us."

Tsizmelia's Plot in the Teratura

Tsizmelia starts. "Sometimes I just feel inhibited by the Cowav."

"You are," Ssflora said. "I participated in a study last year that showed the parts of our brains not connecting with the Cowav: our amgyada, affecting our emotions; our ciritci, affecting our pain and pleasure; and our pricotex, affecting the organization and control of our brain, were thirty-four percent less active now in the average Arzolan than one hundred years ago. The study would indicate that the Cowav is creating lazy brains."

"Well, I'm glad I hardly ever connected," Psozela said. "I grew up known as Psozela the 'uncowav.'"

"The Zeposze also grew up with a creed to only connect when we had to," Mrik said.

"Maybe that is why we are the ones on the ship who are always doing the creative and different things," Hrlur said.

"This cannot be good," Rsoler added.

"The Cenate knew of this study but decided that the Cowav's logic was more important than the individual's creativity, at least for the overall stability of Arzola," Ssflora said.

"That might be fine for the Cenate, concerned with the stability today," Bruid said. "But it can't be good for the future of Arzola."

"Since we are the young and creative," Arlam said, "we need to be the ones to create a change."

"We have to be careful, however," Trelo said. "The Cowav, by directing our actions for mutual good, has taught us the benefits to ourselves of mutual living, which has made us more secure, aware, and appreciative of our lives. In some ways it protects us from ourselves. Tsizmelia and I just had an experience where, as novice traders, we lost a major part of our trading stock. We were thinking the Cowav would inhibit us, and so we did not connect. If we had connected, the Cowav would have saved us a major blunder."

"That is a concern, Trelo," Tsizmelia said, "but the problem is the members of the Cenate think as representatives of their hereditary orders, and their concern is about the current security of Arzola instead of considering the need to prepare for the future. The Cenate thinking needs to evolve."

"This is all good, but it will be years before any of us can be members of the Cenate," Tsizmelia said. "How can we make a change?"

"We need to counter the lazy mind effect of the Cowav," Ssflora said. "Since the Cowav is just the total of all our cerebral waves, as our minds become less active, the Cowav becomes less active, and with less activity there is consequently less knowledge."

"Let's uncowav," Hrlur said.

"We can start a reformation to have everyone uncowav as much as possible," Tsizmelia said. "We can create a set of directives showing how to connect only for essential facts."

"Let's start Cowav fasting," Rsoler said, "where everyone disconnects from the Cowav at least one day a week."

"This is a lot to think about, so let's go to the Xpys to do some motion and clear our thoughts," Tsizmelia said. "We can think about what we have said and meet again."

Exercises and routines are a part of the lives of every Arzolan, and on the Empyramis the Xpys is where the action is. When they entered the Xpys they passed through an arch that scans their bodies and tells them if any part of their bodies is out of tune. They exercised at their own discretion, but once they went through the arch, they knew which muscles need a tune-up.

The Arzola exercise routine is relatively new. About one hundred years ago, the Cowav was not involved with personal exercises. However, around that time, the physical work performed by Arzolans to maintain their basic needs was mostly replaced by autonomic substitutes. The Cowav organized Arzola so that all physical work needed to maintain the civilization would be done by Arzolans during the ten years between the ages of twenty to thirty. After their work years, they needed something to keep them healthy, and so they started doing exercises and routines that are done by every Arzolan every day, or at least every other day.

The Zeposze developed routines to make the exercising enjoyable and to keep them together. With long fingers on their feet like their hands, swinging from bars was easy and exercised their whole body. Their routines made it fun.

At the Xpys, the Zeposze's first routine is like an obstacle course where some Zeposze are the obstacles, and the others complete the course. Arlam swung to the top and got in a catching position. Rsoler looped around a middle bar to make a hoop while Mrik grabbed a bar in the middle on the other side of Rsoler. Bruid then took flight and glided down to where Tsizmelia was waiting. She grabbed Bruid's feet as he flew toward Arlam, where Tsizmelia grabbed Arlam's hands and was swung up to do a flip, go through Rsoler's hoop, and catch Mrik's hands. She was then able to do another flip and land upright on the ground. Trelo, Ssflora, and Hrlur follow suit. Psozela was up next, and although she was regular about her daily Xpys motions, this routine was something new.

"Psozela, do you think your superlative legs are up for this routine?" Mrik asked.

Psozela responded, "If a mindless Militan can do this, I should have no problem." She grabbed Tsizmelia's feet but was low after her first flip and brushed Rsoler's hoop as she went through. She dropped to the bar below, missing Mrik's hands.

"I guess your legs couldn't help with that routine," Mrik said. "It is our most difficult. You should not have any trouble doing our second one."

"Hrlur, you swing like a Fulution," Arlam said.

"And you think like Cxvulp," Hrlur replied.

"You still approach Xpys with the same hesitance you did when you were a kid," Arlam said.

"I do all my Cowav-suggested muscle flexes, but creating a beautiful piece of art is a more meaningful activity," Hrlur responded.

On the way out of the Xpys, Mrik said to Psozela, "I would like to propose another routine."

"I am intrigued," Psozela responded.

"The stars and galaxies pass by in a visual showcase in the Priyramelo. Ideal for an eluva of sensual pleasures and fanciful contemplations," Mrik proposed.

At the apex of the ship is a clear pyramid room with total celestial visibility for meditation and special times.

"What is the future?" Psozela said.

"No future. You excite me physically and with memories of past adventures. It could be an evening like nothing we have ever had before."

"That does sound exciting. Yes, I would like to create this happening with you."

"I will reserve the room."

"I will create a feast from my garden of my traditional foods that will enchant your taste buds."

Mrik secured the room and waited for Psozela. She arrived with no topper, but she really did not need one. She glowed with beauty and self-awareness.

"Welcome to our private eluva of astonishingly vibrant celestial bodies," Mrik said. "Join me on the cushions here in the center, where we can see this beautiful show and have a glass of my calirs hlyusir."

"This celestial show in some ways reminds me of our ride on the Mirudian River after your bazcum attack," Psozela said, "lying flat on my back and looking up into the branches of the Jagger Jungle, where the light from the torch was reflecting off the different layers of branches and thorns, making a magical array of lights that flickered and moved as the torch flickered and we floated down the river."

"At that time, I was thinking how lucky I was having you with me, fighting that bazcum."

"That was a fight, but I remember lying close to you on that raft and thinking how happy I was that the bazcum did not have his way with you."

"Let us entangle our bodies with a sensual mysuvisx. To touch your body is an ecstasy of delight of my mind's highest pleasure. The vivid celestial surroundings, with the palpitations of your heart, and symbiosis of our thoughts and bodies, entangle me so that I never want to leave."

"Never leaving excites my feelings and stimulates my imagination of entanglement," Psozela said.

Psozela and Mrik spent the evening on a celestial cloud of fanciful excitement created by their mutual mental and physical feeling of fulfillment, conscious of shared gratification.

Proleb, Psozela, Mrik

Psozela wanted to prolong the feelings she had from the night before and also had thoughts about the ripple that she needed to tell Mrik, so she went to his suite. Mrik had felt her desire for connecting and had prepared his special breakfast for two, but before he had a chance to invite her, she arrived.

"Our experience last night took me to a place I have never been before," Mrik said. "I know of no other enjoyment that can compare."

"I have been searching my mind for a way to express my feelings," Psozela said, "but I am at a loss."

"I don't know how we can keep this feeling, but I do not want to lose it."

"Let's enjoy it and see where it travels," Psozela said. "But first we need to deal with your ripple so it does not destroy our existence. I have been thinking about how to maintain Proleb's trust as I probe his thoughts."

"Not an easy task, with the length of your relationship. However, he will probably jump at any opportunity to get you involved, unless he is not involved, in which case he will probably just think you are spending too much time around the Zeposze."

"I am meeting him at the Relux later. Will I see you there?"

"I would not want to miss your latest topper design."

Later at the Relux

"What an eloquent topper, Psozela," Proleb said. "Is that a magenta Blisu feather on a pure white radibu, encircled with a purple lusa?" Proleb asked Psozela as she joined him at the Relux.

Psozela liked catching eyes when she walked into the Relux, and a creative topper always seemed to do it. Proleb wears a more formal topper that indicated his Politan status.

"I designed and put it together myself," Psozela said. "I'm glad you like it."

"I can almost see your childhood coming through in your designs."

"It's my time to play with my imagination."

Proleb greeted Mrik as he came in. "Hi, Mrik. We were just discussing dress in the Relux. Where is your topper?"

Mrik responded, "You guys look great, but I just have never got into dress, and I do not want to be part of the entertainment here tonight."

Mrik always looked good, not because of what he wore, but because of the way he presented himself.

"Proleb, have you recovered from that surfing tumble?" Mrik asked.

Mrik had been curious and aware of Proleb's close relationship with Psozela, but now with his ripple concerns, he was even more perceptive of him. As a Militan, Mrik would not consider Psozela, a Politan, for uniting, but he had a feeling for her and was curious about Proleb's relationship with her.

Proleb responded, "I have recovered, except for my ego. I spent a lot of time surfing when I was a kid, but as a Politan I have not had the opportunities."

"How about a cloblang challenge?" Mrik said.

Proleb responded, "It has been years since I have met a challenge. Do you have a need to express your prowess?"

"Maybe so—or it's just a way to connect with you that does not require fancy dress," Mrik said.

Mrik and Proleb took a seat at the cloblang table, a round disc. They both got on and faced each other. They touched hands and feet. A chime sounded, and they began to push. Mrik dominated, but Proleb deferred Mrik's strong moves by letting his energy go past his body. Proleb was losing the struggle when he flashed a bright light from inside his topper, which startled Mrik and allowed Proleb to push Mrik off the disc.

"You resort to trickery to win," Mrik said.

Proleb responded, "Exactly. 'Win' is the key word."

"I did not expect that from a Politan."

"I am going to the Teratura. My bliss blubs are ripening. Would you like to try some? They are mellow and have a psilocybin twist."

"I'm on call now but would like to try some another time. However, Trelo is over there with Tsizmelia, and I know he would enjoy a psilocybin twist."

Proleb walked over to Trelo. "Mrik said you might enjoy a little psilocybin twist."

"I like the freedom of expression it creates," Trelo said.

"My bliss blubs are ripening. Would you and Tsizmelia like to try some?"

"Sure. Can we meet you there when we are done with our drinks?"

"I will be there."

Mrcabzek Intrusion

Mrcabzek walked by as Trelo and Tsizmelia were finishing their drinks and said, "What is the protocol for joining this conversation?"

Feeling the presence of his Militan hereditary order, he was hoping to be able to talk with Tsizmelia, who was currently speaking with Trelo.

"The protocol is to drop your high-minded attitude and be able to relate to the rest of us," Trelo said.

"I relate like any of the Militan, but we have a lofty heritage that needs representation."

"Just because it is lofty does not mean it is better."

"Okay, boys, let's not make this conversation into a battle," Tsizmelia said.

"A battle—that is a good idea," Mrcabzek said. "How about a bubble battle to establish protocol?"

"I did not grow up in battle mode as you have, but I accept your bubble battle challenge," Trelo said.

"There is a training bubble set up for tomorrow. I will get us a time," Mrcabzek said.

As Mrcabzek left, Tsizmelia asked, "Trelo, what are you doing? Mrcabzek has been flying all his life."

"I know it is dumb, but I used to enjoy battling with my friends when I was a kid. I just did not like his attitude," Trelo said.

"Let's go try a little psilocybin twist with Proleb. That should mellow you out."

The Bubble Battle

"This should be fun," Mrcabzek said. "Let's have one battle, and to the winner goes priority protocol between us."

"Is that because you need priority to be able to speak with ladies who would rather speak with me?" Trelo asked.

"Time to see what type of protocol you have in a battle."

As Trelo was getting into the tiny training ship, it brought back a lot of good memories. Mrik, Arlam, and Trelo spent countless ideal hours battling each other as kids. All Trelo's best strategies seemed to fall short against the speed and agility of Mrik and Arlam, but they had great fun. Trelo just hoped some of those strategies would come back.

As the battle began, Trelo was thinking, *This guy is good. I can't get him off my tail.* He had only one opportunity to best him—the trick he used the only time he beat Mrik and Arlam. He needed to release a little fusa for a visual and mental obstruction as he was nearing the skin of the bubble, then break and hard turn at the same time. This tactic was unusual, so with Mrcabzek not expecting it, Trelo might catch him off guard. Trelo found a perfect opportunity and turned his ship at the last second. Mrcabzek, who was intent on keeping on Trelo's ass, caught the skin of the bubble with his wing, ending the game and giving Trelo the win.

"What was that scent that I smelled that distracted me just before the turn?" Mrcabzek asked.

"They call it 'fusa.' It is something I picked up at the trading post. I can get you some if you want, but I guess you will have to find some other way to get over your awkwardness with ladies," Trelo said.

Invasion of the Light

"Trelo, look at that white light entering the landing bay with the exploratory flight," Mrcabzek said.

"It appears to have gone from the landing bay into the ship with that Militan," Trelo responded.

"That ship just returned from a month-long exploratory flight," Mrcabzek said.

Mrcabzek, realizing the potential harm from this unknown light, immediately cowaved the captain. "Captain, I had just finished a bubble battle and am still in the landing bay. A pure white light entered as the exploratory ship landed. I have never seen anything like this before. It appeared to make its way beyond the loading bay and enter the ship without detection. It could be an intruder."

The captain immediately engaged all defensive shields and posted the message IDENTIFY YOURSELF in interstellar language on all the screens in the ship. He notified the ship of possible intruders.

"Full defensive stance and Trivac loading," the captain ordered.

"Captain, this is Psozela. Just before I jumped into my Trivac shoot, I was in the Relux, and a purple light integrated with my topper. It is acting like it was expressing a symbiosis with my topper, and I have to admit it looks outstanding."

All non-essential ship members jumped into their chutes, loaded onto one of the three Trivac ships, and launched. The attack ship also launched. They all went to the skin of the defensive bubble.

"Captain, can you see this blue light at my station?" Sslonious asked. "It is manipulating my controls."

The captain responded, "Can you gain control?"

"I still have control, but apparently so does this blue light. It does not read as a biolife form. It is definitely wave, but I cannot coordinate any of our communication attempts with it."

"I am surrounded by red light," Mrbrixton said. "I do not feel anything, but there are pressures on my Cowav connection."

"Use every wavelength available," the captain said. "We need to communicate."

"Captain, there is a green light that appears to be trying to get into your command bubble," Psimbrosia said.

"Is the green light all waves, or is there a command center?"

"I see the color, but I'm not able to read the waves, and I cannot find a command center."

"Captain, this is Mszmira of Trivac two. A yellow light has enveloped the inside of our Trivac. It does not seem to have any effect on us, and it seems like it has created a pleasant atmosphere. I would describe its actions as frolicking. In fact, Psozela with her purple topper is swirling with the light. I think you could call it dancing."

"Mszmira, come back to the main ship immediately."

The captain commanded, "Everyone, we are turning out the lights on the entire ship. If you see any light, report immediately. Militan Ship Force, begin total ship scanning with your dark views."

"Captain . . . Captain . . . Captain," Mrbrixton said with increasing urgency. "Sslonious, are you able to communicate with the captain?"

"No, but I can see him through the green haze. He appears to be okay."

"Direct all communications to me till we can connect with the captain."

"Mrbrixton, I am back," the captain said. "I switched to hard line and did not lose control, but we must figure out how to communicate to find out its intent."

"Captain," Sslonious said. "The lights seem to be combining as a white light next to your bubble. Could the image it is making be a door?"

"Let's hope so," the captain said. "Clear an exit path for the light to leave the ship."

"It is gone," Sslonious said.

"Sslonious, are there any lingering effects reported?"

"None that I have found. We appear to be back to normal without any harm, with one minor exception. There is a speckle of purple still with Psozela's topper."

"Good, that will be an experience for the Cowav records. Bring the Trivac ships back, and tell Psozela to keep dancing with her topper. I will be in my suite."

As the captain enters his suite, Mssiopeia is waiting.

"I heard you were dancing with the rainbow," Mssiopeia said in greeting the captain.

"Yes, but I did not go home with my partner," the captain responded. "I came home to my partner instead."

"Your rainbow dance makes me think of our uniting dance. I have always enjoyed swinging with you. However, when we return from this journey, our fifty-year uniting will be ending. It has been a good dance. Even when our steps crossed, our rhythm has flowed smoothly. Your swirls will always be with me, but the Cowav designs a different dance floor for our last one hundred years. As our bodies' dance of desires that brought us together diminishes, our minds' mental maturity has given us a slow dance. Now the final one hundred years of our lives are meant to be total freedom— for creativity, mental stimulation, and preparation for the Pamatrical. However, I will always be available for a slow dance with you."

"Freedom is liberating, but I will be ready for slow dancing with you as well."

Cowav Ripple

Psozela had danced with Proleb and had feelings for him. In the back of her mind, she always thought she would end up uniting with him—not because of a great attraction, but he was the most compatible Politan she thought she could find, and they shared childhood memories. She had literally no information on the ripple of which Mrik was speaking, but she thought Proleb would be receptive to her inquiry, because she remembered when Proleb had approached her in the past about going to a meeting of what he called strong Politans. Psozela knew the type of Politan that Proleb was referring to, and they were not the type she wanted to get involved with. They were not individualists but followers.

"Proleb, how about a game of Phi to pass the afternoon?" Psozela asked.

"That sounds like an enjoyable afternoon," Proleb responded.

"If I remember right, you won the last game, so I'm not going to let you win this one."

"I'm feeling pretty spirited this afternoon. I don't think you have a chance of winning."

"Do you remember my suite is a no-Cowav zone, just the same as my room at home?"

"Yes, I know you do have a personality of individualism."

"I don't want to lose that individualism, but I am getting older, and the stuffy ways of the Politan and the conformity of the Cowav aren't as objectionable as they used to be."

"Does that mean that I won't be seeing that great creativity I love in your topper designs?"

"No, I can't give up that part of my identity, but I am beginning to realize the great benefit of being a Politan, the greatest hereditary order on Arzola."

Psozela hoped that if Proleb were a part of the ripple, her statement would be enough to give him the confidence to approach the subject. They continued playing Phi and talking about what was happening at the Relux and who wore the most attractive topper from the night before, when Proleb asked, "Who do you think has the most ability to control Arzola?"

"The Politan, of course. We were bred for centuries to rule, but that is not relevant any longer, because we are a mutual-living civilization and the Cowav directs us," Psozela said.

"Have you ever thought what it would be like if the Politan ruled Arzola?" Proleb asked.

"I have not had those thoughts."

"Doesn't it seem logical", Proleb asked, "that if you take the Politan ruling ability and water it down by adding all the lesser hereditary orders into the mix that the ability to rule would be decreased?"

"You have a point, but we've been a mutual-living civilization for five hundred and seventy-six years, and the topic is not up for discussion," Psozela said.

"But what if it were up for discussion, would you consider it?"

"Because the Politan have better ruling abilities than the other hereditary groups, it would be a good topic for discussion."

"I have been meeting with a group of Politan," Proleb said. "They also believe this way and are actually doing something beyond discussion. Are you interested in meeting with them?"

"You know that I am not a big fan of groups, but it sounds like a good diversion from this long journey. If you are going, I would certainly consider going with you."

"You will have to keep everything related to the group in total secret. Although they do not meet often, there will be a meeting in nine days, and I will accompany you to the first meeting. The group on the Empyramis is small, but there is a large group in Kufina, so you can feel comfortable being part of a major Politan group."

Psozela was anxious to tell Mrik of her success but waited until the next day. Even though she planned to meet him in secret, she did not know how pervasive the Politan group was, and so did not go straight to Mrik, to prevent detection.

The next day they met in a sillsoqote room in the Teratura. Psozela was excited to tell Mrik, and he was eager to hear the new information she had. This could be the introduction to the group they would need to understand the ripple. Mrik and Psozela spent the rest of the day talking about how she should behave at the next meeting to get as much information as possible and yet not give her true intent.

When the meeting day came, Proleb and Psozela went to one of the rooms in the last circumference of the Relux. Only eight Politans were present, and Psozela knew most of them. But before it began, she received what felt like an interrogation. Although she did not feel good about not telling the truth, she had to respond with some unique answers to allow for her acceptance but camouflage her true beliefs. Psimbrosia was the leader and took control of the meeting right away.

They pulled the curtains on the windows between their group and the rest of the Relux, so they were in complete isolation. Psimbrosia began to speak. "We are the Politan, the proud, the intelligent, and the leaders. We were the main energy behind the creation of the Cowav. If the Cowav were under Politan rule, it would have evolved far more than it has to date. The rest of Arzola is living off our greatness. We need to take care of all Arzolans, but they need to be under our direction. We are the natural leaders but are living in a system that is not reaching our highest level of intelligence and power."

Psozela had to leave the meeting early with Proleb, as he explained. Until she was initiated, she could only be present for the inspirational speech at the beginning.

After they left, they went back to Psozela's suite, where they could talk in confidence.

"What did you think of the meeting?" Proleb asked.

"Psimbrosia has some very powerful ideas," Psozela said. "I was not aware there were so many others that had similar thoughts. What can I do to be a part of this quest?"

"There will be a lot you can do, but first let me say that it is a pleasure to me that you have similar thoughts. However, the group limits information for new supporters until initiation. In the meantime, you cannot mention this to anyone, and it would be good to not spend time around any Biru and Rollum."

"Wasn't it great the way Psimbrosia talks about our superiority?" Proleb asked.

"She definitely makes you feel good about being a Politan," Psozela responded. "How are we going to go about making the change?"

"If you decide to become a part of the movement, you will need to go through an initiation to prove your loyalty, and then you will be told everything."

"I would like to become a part of this movement."

"Good. Your initiation will be to end your friendship with your best Biru and Rollum friends, and as part of the breakup you must explain to them that you are choosing Politans to spend your future time with. Your breakup will be Cowav connected so we can watch their responses. If we see acceptance of your actions, then your initiation is complete. You must design your breakup yourself. Feel free to say negative things about the Biru and Rollum, because this will aid in our efforts."

Psozela assured Proleb that she could do this, but even as everyone at the meeting seemed familiar with and accepting of what Psimbrosia was saying, to Psozela her speech was toxic and if not lies, it was fabrications of truths.

At any rate, her ideas were opposite of the feelings needed for their mutual way of living. It was hard for Psozela to believe that her fellow Politans could accept this, but she knew, now she had infiltrated this group, she had to find out how they were creating the ripple in the Cowav. She got a feel for the group, but there was no discussion about the method they used to affect the Cowav. So, she would have to wait until the next meeting, which was three months away.

Psozela spent the rest of the day with Proleb so that he would feel comfortable with her statements.

Mrik and Bruid met with Psozela the next day. She had learned that there were eight Poloyal members on the Empyramis but a much larger group back on Arzola. She also found that Biru and Rollum were targets, and she would need to have minimal contact if she wished to attend the second meeting. Mrik said that it was time to get the Zeposze involved. They knew they could confide in them, and they would need their help—particularly Ssflora's assistance with the science involved in the Cowav. Mrik contacted each of the Zeposze with a time and place to meet at one of the special rooms in the outskirts of the Teratura. He began the meeting by giving them an overview of what was happening.

"I recently visited my third great grandfather in the Pamatrical," Mrik said. "He told me of a ripple that they had observed in the Cowav. He and all the residents of the Pamatrical have extreme concerns, because if the ripple were to grow, it could potentially cause the end of the Cowav and a second death of the virtual lives in the Pamatrical. I have been entrusted by the Pamatrical Cenate with the task of leveling the ripple before it destroys the Cowav. Bruid and I started, and then because Mrhonorix said that the ripple favored the Politan, we solicited Psozela, who has become our undercover eyes into the group that is behind the ripple."

"Wow, and I thought Arzola was past all the intrigue of our ancestors," Trelo said. "What can we do?"

"We need to find out how they are creating the ripple in the Cowav and then how to combat it," Mrik said. "We are waiting to see if Psozela can get us direct information. Until then we can try and figure out how someone has created a ripple in the Cowav without anyone noticing. Make sure you do not let on to anyone what we are doing."

"I have been to one meeting with the Poloyal group, as they call themselves," Psozela said. "It is hard to believe that a rogue Politan group like this actually exists, but it does. They are spouting false information and false narratives that make you want to believe that the Biru and the Rollum are plotting to take over Arzola and disband all the hereditary orders. The information is hard to believe, but their leader, Psimbrosia, is so charismatic that she rallies and inspires those she is speaking to. I noticed that the other attendees were among the less creative and less self-confident of the Politan and so easily misled, but they are nonetheless still able to carry on their quest. This is a lot to think about, so let's go to the Xpys to do some motion and clear our thoughts."

Origin Explosion

The new challenge to figure out the Cowav ripple excited Ssflora, but while she waited for information from Psozela's second Poloyal meeting, she had a family dinner planned. Her parents had a united suite that was bigger, so Ssflora and her brother went there. She was glad to get together with her brother, mom, and dad. She and her brother had finished their family life with their parents but still enjoyed a warm relationship.

"My resteca berry castella is ready to explode on your taste buds," Ssflora said. "It has simmered all day, and the resteca berries are from my first harvest, but let's start with some Ojelos hlyusir."

"This is the best resteca berry castella I have ever had," Ssflora's dad said. "Although I would put a little sizfer sauce in to give a little pizzazz."

"I didn't want to minimize the essential resteca flavors, but I will keep your preference in mind, Dad," Ssflora responded.

Sslonious, Ssflora's mom, asked Ssflora, "How was your day?"

"I spent the day getting beat about by Mrik and others. Mrik is teaching alien self-defense, and my Scienctan blood is feeling like a Militan after today's workout. I just hope I do not have to use what he is teaching us on this trip."

"I hope so, too; however, we had to adjust our path today, because the estimated expansion of the Eluthian Black Hole exceeds our estimates," Sslonious said.

"That supports my personal theory that the black-hole mass accumulation is expanding more quickly than commonly believed," Ssflora said. "I predict the next Origin Explosion will happen in my lifetime. It could be in a blink, so quick we will not see it or know it. The Eluthian Black Hole is just a part of the accumulation of all the matter in the universe."

"The Cowav projects it will not be for at least another million years. It's been thirteen-point-seven billion years since the last one. Why would you estimate it will happen so quickly?"

"We know the expansion of the universe has almost run its course," Ssflora said. "What we don't know is when the contraction will start or how long it will take. Possibly in the blink of an eye. The two opposing forces, the Black Hole attraction pulling inward and the Vacuum outside the universe pulling outward, are getting close to equilibrium. As the universe gets bigger, it reduces the density, which reduces the strength of the Vacuum.

"At the same time, the Black Hole accumulation is getting bigger and stronger. There will be an equilibrium reached when the dwindling Vacuum force equals the increasing Black Hole force, and that is when the direction turns inward toward the Origin Explosion. The Black Hole accumulation will get faster and faster until it is faster than any speed we can comprehend. The speed and accumulation of all the black holes and galaxies of the whole universe combining with such force in one place will be of such a gargantuan amount that it can do nothing but explode, creating the next Origin Explosion and a new cycle for another thirteen-point-seven billion years. History does not give us an understanding of how fast this could happen. The Cowav does not have information on the Origin Cycle, since nothing lives through an Origin Explosion, but we do know that we only have until then to live."

"Let's hope your timing is wrong, but in case you're right, let's party tonight," Sslonious said.

"Have another glass of Ojelos hlyusir," Ssflora said.

"Yes, but I'm meeting with the Sixate in the morning to plan for planet discovery. Are you considering visiting a planet?"

"I've been thinking about it, but I want to get an idea of the planets we will be visiting. I hope you can find some interesting planets."

Sixate Planet Meeting

The captain commanded the attention of the six members of the Sixate so that Sslonious could begin her planetary visit report.

"We have a preliminary journey map from the Cowav," Sslonious said. "It is a good itinerary, but it is probably the safest one we could follow. As an alternate, we could venture into an untraveled area and then return to follow the Cowav map for our planet visitations. This untraveled area is not charted on any map. It would only shorten our planet visits by one fourth solar rotation and give us the opportunity to search a truly unknown part of our galaxy."

"What does your analysis of the Cowav planet visitation selections show?" Trmur asked.

"I have found one planet I think we should substitute, because it would provide more unknown possibilities. It is in the Jiluma solar system, the third planet from its sun. Its origin should indicate an oxygen/nitrogen atmosphere and inanimate life with the possibility of animated life. It is three million, two hundred eleven thousand, seven hundred eighty-three galwaves from origin and two thousand, three hundred fifty-six galwaves from Arzola," Sslonious said.

The captain responded, "Have the Originators been there?"

"One of our expeditions visited another solar system close to the Jiluma solar system fifty-six years ago, and the Originators had been there, so we can assume they had also visited this planet, which I am calling Jrath."

"Thank you, Sslonious. An uncharted area sounds stimulating. Continue with the test waves. I will convene a second planet selection meeting for the Sixate in two days to give us time to review your report and then make a decision."

The Hyper Web

Recently Mrik had begun walking by Psozela's garden on the way to his garden, and today she was there. After greeting her, he said, "The Sixate has selected planets for visitation. Does living on a primitive planet for eight years have any appeal to you?"

Psozela responded, "It does sound adventurous. If you are applying, I would definitely consider it."

"It is hard for me to say this, but I don't want to go if you do not go."

"I feel the same way. We should have the Cowav ripple solved by then, so let's go to a planet. It will be another great adventure.

"Wooooooooooo! Thanks for catching me."

"I thought you just had a sudden urge to be close to me," Mrik said, releasing her.

Psozela smiled. "I guess my urge needed a little assistance, and that jolt surely provided it."

Mrik glanced about. "I have never felt a jolt to the ship like that before. Let's go to my suite and wait for information."

At his work desk in his suite, the captain felt the jolt and immediately contacted Sslonious.

"Sslonious, what just happened?" he asked.

"We are stopping. Looks like we are caught in a hyper web," Sslonious said.

The captain responded, "I'm on my way."

The captain jumped into his tube, which leads directly from his suite to his command center, where his safety bubble activates. His bubble is in the middle of the command center in the heart of the ship, the most protected place on the Empyramis. He stands on a small platform and has a movable control panel that gives him control of all battle essentials. He can see three hundred and sixty degrees in all directions with the surrounding continuous screens in layers showing the vision outside at different distances. It's as if he were in space outside the ship and could freely visualize all directions and get instant magnification. From his bubble he can control the battle by himself; however, his crew usually controls the battle as he directs.

"This type of web is not in the Cowav," Sslonious said. "I have not located the predator yet, but there appears to be one webpower supporting it."

"Mrbrixton, issue a Trivac alert," the captain said.

Members throughout the ship jumped into tubes that took them directly to their Trivac ships.

The captain's voice was heard throughout the ship. "This is not a drill. We are facing a real enemy that is trying to ensnare us."

Everyone seemed to flow smoothly into their designated place, and as the last members slipped into their seats, the Trivac ships left. The Empyramis turned one hundred and eighty degrees to try and minimize the grasp of the hyper web.

Sslonious reported, "We still have not detected the predator, but the Trivac ships have launched. The webs of the hyper web appear to be big enough at this location so that if the Trivac go slow, they can maneuver between the webs."

"Send probes to the webpower," the captain said.

"The predator is now visible, about thirty minutes away, but no identifying characteristics."

"The probes are responding," Mrbrixton reported. "The webpower appears to be the source of the energy, and the webs get ever closer as the they approach the webpower."

"Try all offensive weapons to destroy the webpower," the captain said.

"Captain, we are trying everything. Our weapons just seem to add energy to the web defense."

"Is the web separated from the webpower?"

"No, but if we could get to the webpower, we might be able to destroy it."

"How big are the spaces between the webs?"

"Not big enough to get any kind of a ship through, but a person could possibly get through."

"Are there any waves in the area?"

"There are low-variable waves flowing through the webpower."

The captain connected with Mrik. "Mrik, who is the next best priboarder on the ship after you?"

Mrik responded, "Psozela."

"I need you and Psozela to report to the main ship as quickly as possible with your priboards."

The captain met them on the deck and said, "This is my first experience with a hyper web, and we have tried all defenses that appear in the Cowav to no avail. We only have minutes until we are at the mercy of this web master. The web is protected by one power source. It detects fighters and closes to prevent them from entering, and it casts a shield when weapons are fired at it. My thought is something smaller than a fighter with no propulsion might be able to approach it without setting off its defenses. Riding a priboard might allow you to approach and set a charge. You could use a lasso to draw the explosives into the webpower. Psozela, this would usually be a task for a Militan. Mrik has great faith in your priboard abilities, which will be crucial. Are you willing to accept this dangerous task?"

"I would rather die on a priboard than at the hand of a hyper web master."

"The waves are mellow, but do not touch the webs. We are not sure what they are and what they would do if you touched them. The hard part is going to be getting back. The plan is to have the ship radiate reverse waves to ride back, and if it takes too long, you will have to endure the explosion to get back. If that happens, make sure you are in line with the ship's net."

Mrik said to Psozela, "This is just going to be another tuble geyser ride."

"If you can keep your mind from thinking about the pleasure of touching my legs," Psozela said.

"And you keep from thinking about your next topper design."

"A hyper web topper—that would be interesting."

"Let's try and stay close so we have good cerebral connection. Three, two, one, jump!"

#The webs' spacing is getting smaller. I'm not sure we have enough room to get between the webs.#

#I think I better do the circumference,# Psozela cerebral waved. #I am smaller and can get through those small webs more easily. Give me the lanyard.#

#I would like to challenge you on that, but I do remember your tuble geyser flips.#

#I will round the webpower and tack the waves to get as far back as I can. Get as close to me as you can so I can extend the lanyard to you, and you can pull me back.#

#Nice tacking. Now let's pull the explosives in tight and have the ship start the reserve waves.#

Sslonious reported, "The predator is now eight minutes away, and it appears there is a whole array of ships, although I cannot decipher their origin."

"Have the Trivacs return to the main ship. Prepare for the detonation of the explosives," the captain said.

Sslonious responded, "The predator is now four minutes away. I have tried every means of communicating, and they have not responded. They must be aggressively hostile, setting traps in deep space. We don't know what the predator's weaponry is, and we could come under attack at any time. It is time to detonate and hope Mrik and Psozela are able to get close enough."

"Hold on the detonation," the captain said.

Mrik communicated to the ship, "Go ahead and ignite."

Sslonious reported, "Three minutes."

The captain commanded, "Wait two minutes and then detonate."

#When this wave hits, it is going to be like nothing we have ever experienced,# Mrik waved. #We just need to get aligned with the back of the ship, to get caught by the net. Grab this rope and tie it around you. Wherever we end up, we will be together.#

The instant Mrik saw the brilliant flare of light he grabbed for Psozela, thinking if this was going to be his last breath, she was the person he wanted to spend it with.

Then the colossal force hit, and the explosion created an instant of total unconsciousness for the priboarders. Not that they were not conscious, but the sensory input from the sudden shock, wind, force, and heat left them out of control of their physical and mental awareness. They came back into their senses as they felt the net pulling them into the ship. They were both there and alive.

Sslonious reported, "We are free, and they are back."

"Jumpstart ahead," the captain commanded.

Sslonious reported, "The predator has stopped. Apparently, they are assessing the situation."

At the Relux

"Thank you to our priboard saviors. That must have been a hell of a ride," Arlam said to Mrik and Psozela as they entered the Relux together.

"Yes, it was, and if we had missed that net, we would still be riding," Psozela said.

"It was a great adventure, but Psozela and I have been talking about another great adventure. How about the Zeposze spending eight years on a planet?" Mrik asked.

"You mean spend eight years with beings not concerned about anything beyond themselves," Bruid said.

Hrlur was excited and responded, "But we could be and do anything we want. I'm in, but we would have to come up with a plan to win the stay."

"I'm in too, and who better than the Zeposze to come up with an outstanding plan?" Rsoler said.

"Let's think about this and make a decision next time we meet," Tsizmelia said.

Psozela's Second Ripple Meeting

It had been a couple of weeks since the escape from the hyper web, and Mrik and Psozela had time to prepare for her initiation meeting with the Poloyal. The meeting was held in one of the secluded rooms in the fourth circumference of the Relux, where they are not typically noticed going in and out, and they are completely isolated.

At the meeting, Psozela was asked to come to the front of the room, where Psimbrosia addressed her.

"Psozela, welcome to the Poloyal. We have seen the termination of your friendship with your Biru and Rollum friends," Psimbrosia said. "This proves to us that you are sincere about helping us establish the true position of the Politan at the head of Arzola. Please understand that by becoming part of the Poloyal you are accepting the trust and safety of all of us here and back on Arzola. We are not sure what would happen to us if we were found out before our plan comes to completion. You are now part of a movement that will forever change Arzola and create a better life for us all.

"Now that you are a part of us, let me explain what we are doing. The Politan have always been the noblest hereditary order. We have the most experience and knowledge for governing Arzola. Life will be better once we are in charge and directing the Cowav and have eliminated mutual living. The Biru and Rollum input to the Cowav will only be a drag on the advancement of the Arzola Cowav, and we need to subjugate them so that they will not get in the way of our evolution."

"That sounds like a worthy goal, but with the Cowav in control, how can we accomplish this?" Psozela asked.

"We are creating a ripple in the Cowav, which will develop into a wave that will become big enough to lap and break down the usual patterns of governance. Then the Politan will step in to take control. To create the ripple, we are leading the Cowav in the direction we want. We know how the Cowav collects and organizes information to serve all members of our mutual life. What we are doing is creating false narratives that we are entering into the Cowav with conversations among ourselves and in the neutral narrative. We also create false narratives that are spread and then accumulate in the Cowav."

"Can you show me how I can do this so that I may become a part of this effort?" Psozela asked.

"Yes, we will show you," Psimbrosia responded, "and we are also going to show you how to help spread negative information about the Biru and the Rollum. There are less of them, and they are different. It is easier to create bias in Arzolans' minds about their equality. Once we have created doubt, it is an easy step to convince them there is a reason to evolve in a different direction, away from mutual living and toward an intelligent Politan rule."

"Is there an overall plan that gives us hope that we might succeed?"

"We have found a weakness in the Cowav. Establishment of the Cowav assumed that all the information entered would be truthful, because everyone wanted it to succeed and did not even consider false information. The Poloyal is taking advantage of this Cowav innocence to enter false information into the Cowav so it will conclude the Politan should be in charge. Then we can take control and make changes."

When the second meeting finished, Psozela, newly initiated and excited, met with Mrik—only this time the whole Zeposze was present. She began by giving a little background so the Zeposze would understand how something so egregious could happen.

"When the Cowav started," Psozela said, "all Arzolans were made equal, but the Politan, considered by many to be the superior hereditary order, felt slighted. It is those ancient feelings the new demagogues are playing on, and they have found a way to hijack the Cowav.

"The Cowav usually enters all information with the identity of the Arzolan cerebral waves. However, the Politan have found a way to enter information without exposing their identity. The Cowav programming does not look for false narratives or sort for truth. The Poloyal exploit these entries into the Cowav to build up its false claim of superiority. They are gradually stuffing the Cowav with false information, which it uses to make all the decisions that manage our planet. It has apparently been going on for a long time, because there is enough disturbance for the Pamatrical to notice a ripple.

"Once the ripple becomes a wave and laps, it will cause the Cowav to make prejudiced decisions and conclude that the Politan are best to control the Cowav. Then they step in and do away with our mutual living.

"Psimbrosia is an excellent demagogue and is spreading false information and facts to the Poloyal members who are lacking in self-confidence. They are latching onto these falsehoods to give themselves a feeling of self-importance. She is also using Biru and Rollum to give the weak Poloyal a way to feel good by feeling better than others."

Thinking of Psozela's comments and looking for solutions, Mrik said, "We could bring this information to the Cenate, but with the veto power of each hereditary order, it would not take action, and our efforts would be exposed. The ripple is based on false information stored in the Cowav. We need to access this information and correct it."

"It will not be easy to access this false information," Ssflora said. "To get started, let me explain how the Cowav works. The Cowav has different levels of information. The FACT level collects, processes, and stores information as we interact. It sees all our conversations and actions through our cerebral waves. It does not see what our eyes see, only those visions that our minds choose to record. The ORGANIZE level of the Cowav is where it organizes and categorizes all the information that it collects.

"The ANALYTIC level is where it uses analysis and algorithms to develop conclusions and create directions. The DIRECTIVE level contains the directive, 'The Greatest Happiness for all Arzolans.'

"All the other levels must sync with the DIRECTIVE level. The ripple is currently in the ORGANIZE level, where it arranges the false information along with all the other information. Once it accumulates enough false information, the Cowav will use it in the ANALYTIC level to indicate that Politan rule can provide 'The Greatest Happiness for all Arzolans.' The Politan would then take rule, and the only way to reverse this change would be war between the hereditary orders. We must figure out a way to prevent the ripple from getting to the ANALYTIC level."

Proleb's Attack

It had been a week since Psozela's initiation meeting with the Poloyal, and Proleb was walking though the Teratura. He saw Bruid and Rsoler coming out of a sillsoqote, and then, shortly after, Psozela came out. Proleb ducked out of sight but knew something was wrong. He was hoping for an explanation but could not tell anyone, because he is the one who vouched for Psozela. He waited for a day and then saw Psozela at her garden and invited her to his suite.

"Psozela," Proleb said, "I saw you walking out of a sillsoqote in the Teratura shortly after a Biru and a Rollum.

You have not been truthful with me. Are you some kind of spy?"

"Of course not. How could you think that?" Psozela asked.

"Psozela," Proleb said, "I cannot believe you. Why have you forsaken me?"

"You must have seen someone that looked similar to me."

"There is no mistaking your topper. What am I going to do with you? You have betrayed the Poloyal, and because I vouched for you, they expect me to silence you."

"What does that mean?"

"That all depends on you, but I cannot let you go until it is resolved."

"Okay. I admit I do not believe in the cause of the Poloyal, but you can't just keep me imprisoned in your suite."

"Why not? You have no routine. No one will miss you. They will just think you are on another of your many adventures. I just have to figure out what to do with you until you can see the light in the Poloyal mission."

"How can you side with this small group with a demagogue leader and not me, who has been part of your life since you can remember?"

"Politan are born to lead. The mutual living just waters down our existence. Would you rather be a leader of Arzola, or just another cog in the Cowav wheel?"

"You are letting your basic instinct rule you instead of your cerebral consciousness. You are evolving backwards just so you can feel better than others. Everyone must be equal, or the morality that justifies our lives and directs our mutual life cannot exist."

"The Politan are the best at defining morality, and with the Politan leading, mutual life will not be necessary."

"Why have you forsaken me and all of Arzola?" Psozela asked.

"I am working to make Arzola better for all of us."

"The Poloyal demagogue is using emotionally wrought false information to appeal to your basic self-preservation instinct. Putting one group in charge, even if their instincts for leadership are better, would leave everyone else without the feeling of equality and create a natural imbalance that would eventually result in internal conflict and war."

"We might need a war to make Arzola better."

"You always were a follower, Proleb. It is time to start thinking for yourself. Don't let these few rebels lead you down a path that is contrary to what your basic beliefs have always been."

"I am sorry for your confinement, but I cannot let you go until you see the light and join us for real."

"What are you going to do if I do not convert?"

"That is not an option. I just have to figure out how to make you understand."

"The option is for you to turn from the Poloyal."

"Even if I wanted to turn away from the Poloyal, it is too late. I am committed to the liberation of Arzola. Come into my bedroom. I want to show you a picture I have of us when we were kids."

No sooner had Psozela crossed the threshold of the bedroom than she felt a push on her back and heard the door close behind her. As she lay on the floor recovering from Proleb's push, she was thinking she had never experienced this behavior from anyone, let alone her good friend. He had not only tricked her and physically assaulted her, but now he had her confined in a room that was made for sound insulation and no contact with the outside.

Mrik noticed Psozela missing and started to look for her. He checked with the Zeposze, but no one had seen her. He could not understand how she could be missing on the ship, but a few days had passed since he had seen her, and his concern grew. He could not make a public notice without exposing her Poloyal ripple endeavors, so he began with casual conversation with her mother and sister, each of whom had not seen her. This was extremely unusual, and Mrik began imagining the worst.

All his thoughts kept leading back to Proleb, so he started casually following him. If he was not the answer to Psozela's disappearance, then Mrik did not want to give up their clandestine efforts to understand the Poloyal. But his concern for Psozela got the best of him, so he waited outside Proleb's suite door so Proleb could not see him. As Proleb entered, Mrik followed behind him. There was an immediate fight, as Proleb knew he could not let Mrik in without being found out, and neither wanted to notify the ship's security. Mrik thought that once he entered Proleb's suite he would see Psozela and that would end the search, but Psozela's screams from behind the locked door could not be heard. Proleb grabbed a knife and lunged at Mrik. Mrik dodged Proleb's lunge and grabbed a chair that he swung as Proleb backed away. Proleb went for his control area, where he found dark vision glasses and turned out the lights.

Now Mrik was fighting without vision in a room that he could only see in his memory. He became silent. Now Proleb's motions would be Mrik's vision. As Proleb swung his knife, Mrik heard the movement and moved, but not quite far enough. He felt a sharp cut across his belly, which signaled his time to swing the chair. He could feel it connecting, and he knew Proleb had to be off balance. He lunged toward where he had felt the chair connect, grabbed Proleb, and tumbled to the floor.

He shifted his whole body to control the arm with the knife, and as Proleb beat on Mrik's back, Mrik was able to pry the knife from his hand and quickly turn and knock the dark vision glasses from his face.

Now it was an even fight, except Mrik, a Militan, had spent his whole life training for the fight. Even so, Proleb was able to escape Mrik's grip and, knowing where items were located, started throwing things at Mrik.

Mrik was not able to see Proleb but could hear projectiles flying around the room. Mrik ducked to find something for protection and then listened for the location of sounds. He knew that if he could get the lights back on, he would have the advantage. But in the darkness, Proleb knew where everything was located, and stumbling for a light switch would expose Mrik to Proleb. Silence would have to be his defense. Then Mrik heard what sounded like fingers on the floor—probably Proleb looking for the knife. Mrik lunged and hit Proleb's legs, and it became a wrestling match in the dark.

Mrik attempted to get to Proleb's body as Proleb kicked his legs. Without any weapons, the fight came down to strength, and Mrik could subdue Proleb.

"What are you doing attacking me in my suite?" Proleb snarled. "You will have the harshest punishment."

"Where is Psozela?" Mrik demanded.

"Are you a love-struck fanatic? Is that what this attack is about?"

"Open your bedroom door."

"That is my private place. You shall never enter that."

Proleb paused and then voice-commanded to turn on the lights.

"It's time you leave now," Proleb said.

Mrik had his Militan security belt on under his shirt, which he controlled with his cerebral waves to start his recorder.

"I'm not leaving until you open your bedroom door. All you have to do is open the door."

"I will not open the bedroom door, you must leave."

Mrik quickly isolated Proleb's words "open the bedroom door" on his recorder, and the bedroom door opened. Mrik jumped for the opening before Proleb had a chance to close it. He could see Psozela, but he could not leave the doorway entrance, because then Proleb might close it and confine them both.

Proleb was now free from Mrik's restraint and realized the exposure of his actions. As he was pondering his next move, Mrik quickly pulled a sifer from his belt and slammed it at the bottom of the door to prevent it from closing.

Proleb went for the knife, this time leaving the lights on. Mrik went for Psozela, but Proleb was on him before he could free her. Mrik was forced to do a quick evasion move to escape Proleb's lunge. He backed away as Proleb kept advancing and wildly slicing at Mrik.

Mrik grabbed a plate on the counter to use as a shield but kept backing away around the suite. Proleb slowed for a minute, thinking of how to get at Mrik, giving Mrik a chance to hurl the plate straight at Proleb's head. It struck him in the face. Not enough to seriously damage Proleb, but it gave Mrik a second to lunge for the knife. Then they were on the ground struggling over it. Again, Mrik was able to subdue Proleb, but this time with Proleb's kidnapping of Psozela exposed.

"Are you okay?" Mrik asked Psozela as he released her from the confinements Proleb had placed on her.

"I am fine, but Proleb, what are we going to do with you?"

"You can both join me in making Arzola a better place for all of us," Proleb said.

"Lies and false information persuaded you that Arzola would be better," Psozela said. "You need to escape that imaginative theory and remember reality. In the short run, if Poloyal gained control, you might have greater self-satisfaction through doing things for yourself and receiving more than everyone else, but you would be creating a hostile environment where everyone does not work for a common goal, and in the long run you would not be happy living in that environment.

"Evolution has shown that when we work for a common goal and give up our self-directed lives that life for everyone is better," she reminded him. "We have lived with peace and tranquility, and life has been enjoyable since the beginning of the Cowav. Before Cowav there was always conflict as everyone tried to make life better for themselves by following their basic instincts instead of mutual living."

"Psimbrosia has shown how Arzola would be better for all if the Politan would rule," Proleb said.

"But only a fool could believe that a civilization built on the inequality of its members would be better in the long run," Psozela said. "Inequality spreads discontent, which creates conflicts and will make life less enjoyable for everyone, including the Politan."

The best solution to the predicament that Psozela and Mrik found themselves in would be for Proleb to join them in their quest to expose or control Poloyal, but after the brief conversation they realized that was not going to happen. At least not right away.

They had to devise a plan. Psozela's absence for a couple of days was a concern, especially since Mrik had been asking, so she needed to make an appearance to ease any suspicions. Mrik stayed with Proleb in his suite and continued his conversation with him about his thoughts on the Poloyal.

Psozela mingled around the ship as if nothing had happened and was able to ease some concerns. She then returned to Proleb's suite and joined the discussion. Mrik had restrained Proleb's arms so that he could not hurt them but was free to move within the suite and talk openly.

It was hard convincing Proleb, because Psimbrosia's lies and false information had allowed him to revert to his basic self-preservation and self-preference instinct to create a false scenario that supported Poloyal's plan. They had to go back before the Cowav and remind him that life today was pleasant for everyone because of their mutual way of living.

"Proleb, do you not remember those stories of Arzola before mutual living?" Psozela asked him. "Remember when the leader of the Militan and Politan hereditary groups caused a world war in which there were thousands of deaths, just because they wanted to improve their own position in life?"

Mrik and Psozela took turns talking with Proleb, maintaining their presence on the ship as needed.

"Proleb," Mrik said, "think about what it would be like if mutual living ended. Every time someone did something for you, you would have to consider their ulterior motive, knowing they direct everything to improve their own life at the expense of any other person's life, whereas now everyone is looking out for everyone else's best interest."

Psozela gave Proleb an example. "Remember the story of Srfabio, who convinced his neighbor to help him build a fence between their properties because he knew of a coming storm? Srfabio knew the fence would leave debris on his neighbor's land and not his. The neighbor did not know of the storm, but when he saw the debris after the storm, he realized Srfabio had designed the fence to benefit himself, knowing it would hurt his neighbor. This type of behavior would not happen in a mutual living civilization."

Psozela gave Proleb another example. "Remember the story of the two towns. One had no organization, and the Arzolans did everything for themselves, and the other was organized by mutual living. At first, the town without organization seemed a benefit, because you could do whatever seemed best for each individual, until there was a shortage of bread. There was conflict for the bread, and everyone had their own efforts to get more bread, which created fighting and discord. Everyone ended up leaving the town. The mutual town just divided up the bread equally, and life went on with a little less bread but a feeling of comradery.

They also reminded Proleb that before they evolved, there was conflict, discontent, hardship, and life was not pleasant.

It took them two days with Proleb before they started to see some light in his thinking. They could not push their beliefs on him, so it was taking time to reformulate his thinking that had been developing over the past couple of years.

Eventually he came around of his own volition, and now they had to start thinking about revising their actions with the Poloyal. Proleb provided much more information and was a great aid to Ssflora as their efforts to counter the ripple continued.

The Uniting

Trelo waited for Tsizmelia to arrive at the Priyramelo, controlling his excitement. He had something of upmost importance to ask her, so as soon as she arrived, he started right in.

"Tsizmelia, you are stable, strong, and as bright as the morning sun," Trelo said. "You are kind, patient, and as beautiful as the evening moon. You have been the female of my desire since I became aware that you could be more than just another friend. I would like to spend my united life with you and raise a family."

"I have been waiting a long time for this day. I could not imagine uniting with anyone but you," Tsizmelia said. "And you could not have picked a better place to ask than here at the apex of the Empyramis, with total visibility of the galaxy as we travel on our incredible journey."

"Now we can start thinking about the Uniting Exhibit," Trelo said.

"I have always looked forward to the uniting ceremony but have questioned my ability for the exhibit. It is so beautiful and meaningful, the way a couple swing around the bars and then join on the last swing together as if to illustrate that their free swings are now combining into a double swing to be as one."

"Practicing for the Exhibit is not going to be easy," Trelo said. "I guess it is a good test of our resolve to be together. I suppose it can be seen as a practice in working through difficult tasks as a couple. It will be a good statement of our resolve to be together."

The Uniting Exhibit is a physical and beautiful display by a uniting couple. It is difficult to do and takes much practice. If the pair does not end together at the same time, it is taken as a sign, they are not ready, and tradition dictates they are not to unite or try again for another year.

Trelo and Tsizmelia committed to each other and began practicing for the Uniting Exhibit. They made arrangements for the Exhibit and the celebrations after.

The Exhibit would be held in the Xpys, where they could exhibit, then moved to the Relux for a big celebration.

Mrik was in the Relux with Psozela when he heard the news about Trelo and Tsizmelia's commitment.

"Everyone always expected Trelo and Tsizmelia to be united," Mrik said. "I can't wait to see their kids. Have you started looking for a Politan uniting partner?"

"I always thought it would be Proleb," Psozela said. "But now that he got involved in the Poloyal, I have to work through that. I always knew he was a follower, but I would have to get past the fact that he was actually trying to kill you. Have you started thinking about uniting?"

"I always thought that I would know right off when I met the right Militan, but it just hasn't happened," Mrik said.

Time passes by slowly on the journey, but Trelo and Tsizmelia's uniting ceremonies seemed to come quickly. The Xpys was not as large or ornate as the usual Uniting Exhibit theater, but it had the space and the bars. Trelo and Tsizmelia both sprang from opposite ends of the chamber.

Tsizmelia was wearing a gown that had numerous free-flowing parts that followed her motions through the bars, creating a vision of soft, delicate swirls around the bars. Trelo with his formal but snug clothing seemed to bounce in and out between Tsizmelia's tailings. Each had their ceremonial Tradan toppers, and although they added to the pomp of the Exhibit, they also added to the difficulty of the motion. Trelo and Tsizmelia's excitement must have carried them through, because with all the difficulties of the Exhibit, their motions were precise, with beauty and calm. They ended by coming down together at the exact same time, right next to each other.

Mirk and Psozela saw the delightful moment and although they were not together, their eyes connected. For an instant there was an unspoken feeling, *This should be us.*

As Trelo and Tsizmelia landed, all the parties of the celebration crowded around, embracing their Uniting. It was beautiful, and then Trelo and Tsizmelia's friends and family carried them to the Relux, where a planned celebration took place. The whole ship attended.

The Originators

"Your zelas are bursting out of their buds," Arlam said.

"The best of my garden. I'll get you some once they are ripe," Ssflora said.

"You know you are going to have to step up your topper design if you want to catch eyes in the Relux when Psozela is present," Arlam said.

"She is a big-city Politan and is all about show and appearance. She is from a different reality than what we experienced in Ciles. I'm happy being a Ciles Scienctan."

"What do you think of the Zeposze's Jrath plan?"

"Well, I would not have to think about topper designs. Jrath does seem like it is an interesting planet. The Sixate report suggests the Originators probably seeded for the bipedalintellect beings on Jrath about six million years ago. A little after they seeded Arzola."

"I wish we knew more about the Originators," Arlam said.

"They are probably in some other corner of the universe. By the nature of their expeditions, they must have wanted to create species similarities from one solar system to the next. They sure did a lot toward making the bipedalintellect beings the main evolutionary life. Maybe Jrath could provide a clue about their lives."

"Are you thinking about spending the next eight years on Jrath?" Arlam asked.

"It is a hard decision, but if you want to partner on Jrath, we do have a close relationship with no thoughts of uniting. I have investigated Jrath. There should be varied terrain and interesting plants, and the people should not yet be to the warring evolutionary level. My one concern is that eight years is a long time, and I am ending my single age and need to find a suitable Scienctan."

"With your charm and beauty, you can easily find a Scienctan once we return to Arzola. Let's have an eluva tomorrow night and grow our relationship."

"Do you have something in mind?"

"An adventure to the far corners of the ship, through the Teratura and ending in the private garden sillsoqote with a little mysuvisx."

"Good idea before we possibly spend eight years together. But first we have to go to the Zeposze's Jrath meeting."

Zeposze's Jrath Meeting

"Jrath would be an adventure of the unknown," Tsizmelia said. "If we commit to these eight years, there will be no turning back, because the Empyramis will not be back until then. The Sixate has suggested that the Originators have seeded bipedal intellectuals on Jrath, but we have no idea of their evolutionary level."

"There has not been any communication detected from Jrath, so the level is probably primitive," Ssflora said.

"We will have to develop a visitation plan to submit to the Sixate," Rsoler said.

"Bruid and I have been working on a preliminary visitation plan," Psozela said. "I think if we submit our request based on this plan, we will be viewed favorably by the Sixate. The plan is guided by the most important thing we can do, which is to give Jrathlings an awareness of their place in their solar system and the universe and how they can use this knowledge to better their lives.

"We will plan on spreading this awareness around the planet," she explained. "But because we are only allotted one tonxer, we must limit our mega projects. We can use it to build a great pyramid with a galaxceiver. The great pyramid will introduce them to relationships that exist between Jrath and the celestial bodies surrounding it, and it will generate power for the galaxceiver, which will give us the ability to speak with them once we are back on Arzola. We can also build a gravomagnetic resonator that will give them a guide to understanding the universe and those forces that affect them. Building both projects to last for millennia will reveal our presence after we are gone.

"Jrathlings are probably a millennium away from having mutual-life capabilities," Psozela continued. "However, we can present concepts that they probably do not have but will need to create a mutual society. For example, a civilization based on justice, fairness, and equality, and, most important, to understand their own self-preservation instinct and the need to go outside themselves to consider themselves just like everyone else. Understanding evolution to mutual living will take time for them to understand, and mutual living needs participation by everyone for it to work. Their lives are far from being ready to understand. But we can give them a vision with steps to take and signs to follow for the future so they will have a direction once we are gone. Understanding their place in the universe will be the first step and give self-confidence in their own decisions, knowing they are directing their own lives."

"Well stated, Psozela," Bruid said. "We could have four groups with one to build a pyramid for a galaxceiver, one group to build a gravomagnetic resonator, one to spread the knowledge of the skies around Jrath, and one to assist the other three and develop other Jrathlings' original projects."

"Each group would use their livpyramis for travel and security," Mrik said. "Upon arrival we can all travel together around Jrath and do some preliminary readings, observing the climatic, gravomagnetic patterns and the inhabitants."

"Psozela, will you put this all together and submit it to the Sixate?" Trelo asked.

"Yes, with a little Kufina flair."

Bogatars

"Captain, we are about to enter the Volup Corridor, where the Interstellar Map Council has established boundaries," Sslonious said. "The Bogatars claimed the corridor after they were victorious in a war with the Cxvulp. The Interstellar Map Council has not changed the boundary and is hearing protests from neighboring domains, but the Bogatars are enforcing their claim. We can bypass their new space, but it will take an additional week. They have been participating in war in this area, so they might have cruisers in the area."

"How good is their tracking equipment?" the captain asked.

"Our last report shows some weakness, but that report was ten years ago and made by the Cxvulps."

"Identify yourself," said an unknown voice.

The captain answered, "We are the Empyramis from Arzola in the Aolasel solar system. We are traveling to the Jiluma solar system."

"You are in Bogatar territory. Acknowledge submission."

"The interstellar map shows this as disputed area."

"Not disputed by the Bogatar. Acknowledge submission, or you will be destroyed."

"Destruction is of no value to you, and our defenses are quite robust. Perhaps we could discuss a gift for your pleasure."

"What do you have?"

"Some very valuable items from across the galaxy. Come to our ship and look."

"This is Bomax. I will come to your ship to view your valuables."

Speaking to his crew, the captain said, "Full Trivac Alert. Trmur, you will need to do the negotiations with your stockpile of trading goods. We don't know how formidable their weapons are, so try to make them happy.

"We will need to do something to protect ourselves while we let Bomax through our bubble," the captain said.

"We can create a small bubble inside the main bubble," Sslonious said. "I will start working on it."

The Bogatars Arrive on the Ship

Bomax was a bipedalintellect but did not look anything like the Holua. He had large scales on his back and running over his head and down to cover a short tail. He had bright shining beads of metal and gems all over his body that swung as he walked. Although his body was not pleasing to visualize, the metal and gems made for an interesting appearance.

"Bomax, please follow me to our especially valuable cargo vault," Trmur said. "This is a Cxvulp crystalline jewelry set. Isn't it exquisite the way the beautiful, sparkling blue crystals are fixed in the intricate, glimmering setting, and the light travels around and through all the crystals before presenting a brilliant visualization? The most beautiful jewelry you can find anywhere. This is a Fulution brain translator capable of translating all languages in sector five of our galaxy. As you can see, there are more items than I have time to explain. Do any of them attract your attention?"

"I want them all," Bomax said.

"That is not possible. The purpose of our entire mission is to trade these items."

"Well, maybe you can trade yourselves instead." Bomax eyed them with arrogance. "I am going back to my ship. Prepare to have these items transported to my ship, and then you will be free to go." Bomax briefly looked around the room and returned to his ship.

"Captain, an alternative to giving away Trmur's trade would be a quick escape," Sslonious said. "We could accumulate and spark the plates, which would give us a lead on the Bogatars. However, we would need a short delay to escape their initial weapons, and I do not know how long it would take them to catch up."

"When would we be able to initiate a spark?" the captain asked.

"To align the plates and let them accumulate without the Bogatars noticing it would take thirty-five minutes."

"Start immediately."

"Captain of the Empyramis," Bomax summoned from his ship. "Do you have the items ready to transport?"

"Bomax, we cannot give you all the items. We need them for trading, and the Interstellar Council shows this space is in dispute. We are just willing to give you a precious item as a gift to show our appreciation of your friendship."

"We have no friendship for you and will destroy your ship if you do not transfer all the items."

"I think you went back to your ship too quickly. If you come back, I will show you our formidable weaponry, and this could prevent a cataclysmic event between our two civilizations."

"This is agreed. I will review your weaponry, then you will transport all of the goods."

"Sslonious, prepare for Bomax's second visit, and find the closest planet that is big enough to hide the Empyramis. Set a course past that planet with a false itinerary. When Bomax reviews our weaponry, make sure he has access to the itinerary. Our plan will be to show them everything but our GX zasers. We need to give them a false sense of security to gain enough time to get temporarily out of their scanner reach and skirt behind that planet before they can catch up. If they follow, hopefully, they will go with the false itinerary."

"Captain, I had a look at their transporter when they were here last," Mrbrixton said. "There was only one pilot left on the transporter, and it had exterior propulsion. If we could create a distraction and place a controllable cover on the propulsion exhaust, it could greatly reduce Bomax's transport speed and give us a little time to escape."

"Great," the captain said. "Use whomever you need to get the job done."

Mrbrixton reached out to Mrik for assistance. "I need a couple of the best-looking ladies around your age that are on the ship to feed a Bogatar some food."

"You want Psozela and Ssflora," Mrik said. "Where would you like them to meet you?"

"In the entry bay."

"They will be there in five minutes."

"Psozela and Ssflora, meet me in the entry bay as soon as possible," Mrik cowaved.

"What do you want?" Ssflora asked.

"Mrbrixton asked me to have two beautiful women meet him there."

"Thanks for the compliment, but are you going to prostitute us to the Bogatars?" Psozela asked.

"I don't think he is thinking in those terms, but this could be a life-or-death situation."

"Mrbrixton, this is Ssflora and Psozela," Mrik said as they gathered in the entry bay.

"Greetings, and thank you for working with me on this operation," Mrbrixton said. "There is one Bogatar in their transporter. This is his second trip, so he should feel secure. I would like you two to serve him some snacks. The reason for your intervention is to distract him so we can set exhaust covers on his transporter. We have videos of their leader, Bomax, to study his behavior. Think creatively, and I will see you here in ten minutes."

Ten Minutes Later

"We are expecting to have fifteen minutes before they leave, so don't feel panicky about time," Mrbrixton said. "It will take us five minutes, and we will start as soon as you get him into an obstructed position."

"Let's shine some light in his window to get his attention," Ssflora said.

"He is opening the door," Psozela said. "We have brought you some snacks," she said when he stood before them.

"I do not want snacks," the Bogatar said.

"But it is the custom of Arzola to welcome all visitors to our ships," Ssflora said. "It is just something to eat we think you would enjoy."

"Bogatars do not eat for enjoyment."

"Do you spend time with the women of Bogatar?" Psozela asked.

"Women serve only at the pleasure of men."

"We would like to know about the women of Bogatar," Ssflora said. "Could you tell us about your women?"

"Come in, and I will tell you." He stepped aside so they could enter. "Our women are sensual, beautiful, and attentive to our every want. You look sensual."

"These snacks are really quite good, and I will eat first so you do not have to worry about poison," Psozela said.

"You are beautiful. I will touch to see if you are sensual."

"Arzolans talk and eat before touch," Ssflora said. "We have designed this snack to heighten sensual pleasure."

"I am Bolow. You eat this one, this one, and that one, and then I will eat."

"Bolow, do Bogatars live together with their women?" Psozela asked.

"We do, but they do not travel on military missions with us."

"Is this a military mission?" Ssflora asked.

"Yes, we are going to control the universe. I have tasted your snacks. Now I want to taste your sensual being."

"To heighten the sensual experience on Arzola we create an eluva. Let's design an eluva so you can have the maximum gratification."

"On Bogatar men design everything. How would you maximize gratification?"

A ping sounded, and Psozela held up a finger.

"Just one moment. I just received a message from our ship that it is time for our Mutual meditation," Psozela said. "We will be right back after our meditation."

"Tell your Mutual that your meditation has been fulfilled and you are in the good hands of Bolow."

"I'm sure our Mutual will appreciate your good-hands offer," Psozela said.

Psozela and Ssflora turned and left the Bogatar transporter.

"Thank you, Mrbrixton," Ssflora said. "You rescued us just in time. It was starting to get a little hot."

"Good work," Mrbrixton said. "Now it is up to the captain to get us out of here."

"Captain," Mrbrixton said as he connected with the command center, "the exhaust covers are in place."

"Good. Now timing will be critical," the captain said.

As the Bogatar transporter cleared the landing bay, the captain ordered, "Jumpstart. Close the exhaust covers on the Bogatar transporter. Retract the bubble."

"Captain," Sslonious said, "the Bogatar transporter is outside our bubble range."

"Reinflate the bubble and get us to that planet as quick as you can," the captain said.

"It worked," Sslonious said. "It should take Bomax at least three minutes to get back to his ship, and we should be out of scanner range by then."

"We are approaching the planet, Captain," Sslonious said.

"Turn sharply toward the far side of the planet and find a place to land."

The landing was gentle, and the planet was beautiful, with high squiggly mountain ranges showing strips of magenta, orange, yellow, and different shades of brown minerals, creating a collage throughout the terrain. However, it was inhospitable to life, and they did not leave the Empyramis.

"Sslonious, set the bubble to reflect the terrain in case the Bogatars search this planet," the captain said.

"Captain," Sslonious said, "it has been two days. We should be safe to continue if we circumvent the territory the Bogatars are now claiming."

"Keep visual and proceed," the captain said.

Empyramis Living

"Are you in the Teratura to seek solace after your encounter with the Bogatar?" Mrik asked as he passed by Psozela at her garden.

"Getting me involved in these risky adventures is becoming a pattern," Psozela said. "What do you have planned next?"

"Nothing, I hope, but this flight sure is providing adventures beyond my expectations."

Mrlfectori saw Mrik talking to Psozela and walked up to join the conversation. Seeing the gentle breeze that Psozela as using on her catazumies, he attempted to show his wisdom.

"I could create the same effect with a little heavy breathing," Mrlfectori said.

"I'm sure my catazumies would appreciate your heavy breathing," Psozela said. "But it was my grandpa's wisdom that provided me with the knowledge that a little breeze required the folpia to strengthen its overall system, which resulted in a strengthened folpia flavor. I add a little breeze to the afternoon light, and my folpia catazumies are yummy."

"I'll let you two to your gardening," Mrik said as he excused himself.

"Psozela, how about letting me grow a piece of your garden?" Mrlfectori asked.

"Mrlfectori, you are too young to have your own garden. There is a reason for the age limit."

"Yes, I know, but we are on a journey. The normal does not have to apply, and you could enlighten me on realities of life while we garden."

"I have always enjoyed my gardening time, but I am sure I would also enjoy spending time with you. Perhaps it is time for you to experience gardening, but you must understand the reason it is done by older Arzolans. It is a long-term commitment and is meant to provide solace and tranquility."

"I have already developed my plan for creating some very unique and special flavors, and you could watch over me and direct my activities."

Mrlfectori felt he could be as capable as any adult, but he also was at the age where being around an attractive female was enticing.

"Okay, Mrlfectori, you can have a ten ground; however, I will expect twenty percent of your produce, and you must be careful not to do anything that will affect any of my plants. Take that ten ground in that corner."

"Thanks, Psozela. To get me started on the right step, what is the most important thing you can tell me about growing?"

"Most of what you need to know, you will find in the Cowav. The one thing I always strive for is good communication. Your plants will tell you when you are not treating them right. It takes time to learn their language. They will speak through their movements, color, and growth, or lack thereof. If you listen to them long enough, they will let you know what makes them feel best and most productive. Enjoy your ten ground, but right now I need to get into line for Hrlur's polusos berries. You can come along if you want."

"Hi, Hrlur. I am not familiar with how lines work, but I wanted to make sure I get some of your polusos berries. So here I am an hour ahead, and I see I am the only one," Psozela said.

"Hi, Psozela and Mrlfectori," Hrlur greeted them. "I am not sure how lines work either, but my harvest of polusos berries is so popular, it was not big enough to fill all the requests, so I needed to do something. I could have used a lottery or something else, but I thought a line would allow the Arzolans with the biggest desires to show their craving by waiting in line."

"I remember from history in a few times of crisis, lines were common," Psozela said, "but I have never waited in one. We can turn it into a line party."

"That should make my polusos berries even more popular. This is only my tenth harvest, but I have been cultivating these berries all of my life."

"Now it looks like your line is starting to grow, showing the value of your long pursuit."

"Hrlur, I am late, and there are many ahead of me," Arlam said. "I was hoping as a fellow Zeposze you might be able to improve my position?"

"Well, Psozela and Mrlfectori have been here for an hour, and the others for varying amounts of time," Hrlur said. "To give you an advantage would destroy the whole concept of a line, not to mention going against our mutual-living values.

The only way to improve your position is to negotiate a trade with someone who arrived before you."

"Rsoler, if you trade positions with me, I will invite you to a polusos berry party I am planning," Arlam said.

"I've tasted your cooking, Arlam. No, thanks," Rsoler responded.

"Ssflora, it is beautiful the way your topper color matches the shade of the polusos berries," Arlam said.

"Just the way your late arrival matches your lack of concern for the polusos berry, but I would consider an invite to your polusos berry party."

"Mrlfectori, you touch my leg again, and more than your topper will be on the floor," Psozela said as Mrlfectori attempted his naive form of flirting. "You need to get ahold of your teenage hormones. I am going to the Relux to think about your gardening. Do not follow me."

At the Relux

"A Magical Mystery Millium Meander provided by Mrhonorix," Mrik stated as Psozela encountered him in the Relux.

"I still have to talk with Mrhonorix about letting you take me into Mysticwild."

"Actually, he tried to talk me out of going," Mrik said. "He said he would not suggest that adventure to anyone."

"So, what kind of an adventure has he concocted for us now?"

"Imagine your mind floating free with no needs and only sensual stimulation of magical visions and joyous encounters," Mrik said.

"What galaxy are you in?" Psozela asked. "Those lights from the light invasion must have done something to your head."

"While Mrhonorix was trying to talk me out of going to Mysticwild, he told me about a stash of millium he had acquired on one of his adventures. It is a purple flower that has a mind-expanding effect, and although he had only tried it once, he said it was an experience that everyone should have at least once."

"Was Mrhonorix an adventurous journeyer?" Psozela asked.

"Yes, the millium is the product of one of his adventures, and I followed a map he gave me to gather it before our flight. He said eating provided a mind-bending meander that loosened his mind to create freedom and untangle his thoughts. He did not report it and only mentioned it to me because he felt the Cowav might not approve. I have planted the seeds and am attempting to grow them, but I would like to try taking some. Mrhonorix was a little uncertain about the effects because he had only taken it once; however, he did not detect any long-lasting consequences. Ssflora analyzed them for me, and although they have some molecular structures she was not familiar with, there are no toxins. Are you interested?"

"Sounds exhilarating, and although I should know better than to make unknown adventures with you, I would enjoy a little excitement."

"Good. I am on twenty-four-hour strategic call while on this journey. Apparently, we would need to be free of any responsibilities for at least six hours. I'm going to figure out how to arrange the time."

"What would we do for six hours?"

"Explore the inner workings of our minds."

"Sounds stimulating. I'd like to find out what is in your bizarre mind."

"Good. I'm not going to tell anyone of our plan except Arlam, whom I will ask to be our safety in case something goes wrong."

Psozela and Mrik met in Mrik's room.

"Here is your portion," Mrik said.

"How long till it takes effect?" Psozela asked.

"I don't know."

"Let's play some Phi."

Mrik and Psozela sat at a table playing Phi. Some time passed.

"Let's take a walk to the Teratura," Psozela said.

"Feel the leaf of this arberva tree," Mrik said. "You can almost feel the water running through its veins, and it seems to be vibrating as if to say hello."

"Look into the Teratura horizon. Do you see all those displays of different colors and patterns, as if to entice our minds into its fantasy?"

"Look at this plumerine fruit on Tsizmelia's tree."

"It is big and ripe. It feels like it is telling me to take a bite. Oops, it fell off. What do I do now?"

"Well, we do not want to expose our adventure, so let's eat it and hide the seed."

"I can feel Tsizmelia's disappointment," Mrik said. "Oh, but it is so good."

"I'm hungry even though my body does not need food right now."

"What I am thinking is, an eluva would feel really great."

"I don't think we could top the Priyramelo eluva we had, but if we could get the Priyramelo, I surely would like to try with a little help from this millium."

"I will see if it is available. But I am not sure I can do this. Am I talking funny?"

"You always talk funny, Mrik. Let me do this. We are in luck. It is available in an hour, and I have booked it. That just gives us enough time to prepare some catazumie."

"Let's see if we can act normal on our way back to my suite to make the catazumie. Even though I am off duty, I do not want anyone to perceive me as strange."

"Aren't you always naturally strange?" Psozela asked.

"Maybe to someone only concerned about her latest topper design."

Mrik and Psozela make the catazumie and head for the Priyramelo. They are full into the millium effects as they make their way to the Priyramelo with the hot catazumie. Laughing and carrying on as if they were little kids, it was good that they did not run into anyone on the way.

"Look at that array of colors and shapes that are amplifying the galaxies."

"And I have no fear of my thoughts."

"I think we developed feelings from when we were so dependent on each other in Mysticwild," Psozela said.

"I can remember thinking for the first time if something bad was going to happen, I would rather it happen to me than you."

"I don't think I have ever had a complete trust in someone as I did with you on our journey."

"These memories are coming back with great emotions highlighted by this millium."

"These visions are beyond description," Psozela said.

"Your leg feels like the most elegant cluva with the warmth of a ruso wave at prime height. I have never had such an ecstatic feeling that is so tantalizing."

"Your body seems to encompass me in a way that makes me feel so serene and totally aloof of this universe."

Psozela and Mrik spent the balance of their millium adventure exploring each other physically and mentally, looking into the rainbow galaxies, and creating visions and dreams of their greatest creativity.

"It has been a precious evening. When we get back to Arzola, we need to go see Mrhonorix and thank him for the milium," Psozela said.

"This millium should be part of every eluva."

Psozela and Mrik headed back to their suites to recover from their magical millium adventure, but shortly after Mrik arrived at his suite, Tsizmelia was there. Although Mrik's only official position on the Empyramis was commander of one of the Trivac ships, as the only Militan of the Zeposze, he was the one the Zeposze members went to for authoritarian counsel.

"Mrik, someone took a plumerine fruit from my garden," Tsizmelia said.

"Are you sure it didn't ripen and fall to the ground?" Mrik asked.

Mrik probably did not realize it when he replied to Tsizmelia, but he was still experiencing some of the effects of the millium. It accentuated his fear of being caught using the unregistered plant and then taking a fruit from another garden without permission. His quick response led Psozela and him on another journey of fabrications, which was new for both of them. But once started, was hard to stop.

"I am sure. I saw it yesterday and today I checked everywhere it could have been."

"Let's go look. I would like to see this."

Tsizmelia, Psozela, and Mrik headed for the Teratura.

"It was right here, beautiful, purple, and ready to pick."

"Let's get the Zeposze together and try to and solve this mystery. In case this is just a prank, we do not want to get someone into serious trouble."

Zeposze Meet at the Relux

"Someone has picked my plumerine fruit from my garden," Tsizmelia said.

"Are you sure it wasn't your brother?" Hrlur asked.

"I have spoken with my brother, and it was not him," Tsizmelia said.

"Maybe it was Ksia," Rsoler said. "She is the only one on the ship not familiar with our ways."

"I will check with her," Mrik said, "but it does not seem like something she would do."

"Who do you think may have done this?" Trelo asked.

"I do not know. You just do not hear of such things happening," Tsizmelia said. "The disgrace someone would receive would be so extreme."

"Okay, we must create a plan to solve this mystery," Mrik said. "Although there are no visuals in the Teratura, we can check the visuals at the door and see who went in, even though almost everyone on the ship goes to the Teratura at least every other day. Tsizmelia, do you have a time frame to start?"

"I went yesterday at about mid light and about the same time today," Tsizmelia said.

"I will review the Cowav video of the entrance and see if I can find any incriminating information," Psozela said.

"I will peruse the Cowav to see if there is any information that looks suspicious," Trelo said.

"I will go to my garden and talk to the neighbors to see if they noticed anything different," Tsizmelia said.

"I will go with you and see if I can find any evidence from feeling the dirt," Rsoler said.

At Tsizmelia's Plumerine Tree

Rsoler checked out the soil. "There is definitely some disturbance. Here it is, the seed from your plumerine. Let's clean it up and inspect it."

Bruid looked at the seed. "There are two teeth marks. One is strong, and one is weak. They both look like Holua teeth. The strong one must have come from an Athlan or a Militan and the weak from a Politan or a Scienctan."

"Great. Good limiting information, and a little surprising it was two Holua," Tsizmelia said. "It looks like there was a well thought-out plan. Ssflora, please take it to the lab and check for genetic markings."

"Let's set a trap," Hrlur said. "I'll go make a plumerine that looks and feels just like a real one, and we can hang it on the tree."

"I will make an alarm we can put in Hrlur's plumerine to let us know when it is touched," Ssflora said.

"Since we are temporarily keeping this to ourselves, I will act as the collection point," Mrik said. "Communicate to me."

Psozela and Mrik hung back from the Zeposze as they departed.

"I feel so horrible," Mrik said. "I never lie to anyone, let alone the Zeposze."

Psozela responded, "I know. How did we get ourselves into such a predicament, and what do we do about the genetic markings test?"

"I think because we were under the influence of the millium, we were not trusting our own thinking, and without the Cowav, we relied on our primal selfishness. Instead of just explaining to Tsizmelia, which would have been okay with her, our thoughts were just on our own preservation."

"Mrik, Psozela," Mrlfectori said. "I happened to be in my garden when you picked and ate the plumerine. I thought it was strange, but it all came together today when a I saw all of you there finding the seed."

"Yes, I suppose it would seem a little strange," Mrik said.

"There is a seat on your Trivac right next to that young Politan girl. If you were to change my seat next to her, I would not have time to speak with anyone else about such things as seeds."

"Mrlfectori, you know the Cowav assigns those seats for fastest preparation."

"Yes, but you can override the Cowav."

"I will not do that, Mrlfectori."

Mrik and Psozela went to Psozela's suite.

"I can't believe Mrlfectori is extorting us, particularly after I let him grow in part of my garden," Psozela said.

"This has got to stop. It is like an infection and keeps growing," Mrik said. "We have to go to the Zeposze and explain."

Zeposze Meeting

"A confession from Psozela and I with extreme humility. We ate Tsizmelia's plumerine. We were on an experimental millium trip, and the plumerine just seemed to fall into my hand, and because we were being secretive about the millium trip, we thought we should just continue with our secret."

"Okay with me, but when do we get to go on a Zeposze experimental millium trip?" Hrlur asked. "I'm thinking tomorrow would be excellent."

"I'm attempting to grow some, so we will have to wait for my first harvest," Mrik said.

"Tsizmelia, we are so sorry. How can we make this up to you?" Mrik asked.

"The plumerine I could have given to you anyway, but the Plumerine Mystery you helped to perpetuate is hurting. However, I know you well enough to know you did not intend on hurting me, and so I'm looking forward to the Zeposze millium trip."

Mrik and Psozela could understand Tsizmelia's feeling and were dealing with their own remorse as they gave her a hug of friendship and then left.

"Now to deal with Mrlfectori," Mrik said. "Let's check the Teratura."

"Mrlfectori, your conversation about the plumerine was very disconcerting," Mrik said. "Although your comments were not definite, your intent was clear. As a young man you are still developing your personal reality, and you showed a serious lack of understanding of the intent of mutual living: to place others' well-being equal to your own. It was a creative and initiative action, but your lesson here is that the Cowav always trumps yourself. You cannot expect respect until you practice this concept."

"For me, Mrlfectori, it is just disappointing," Psozela said. "You still have growing up to do. I am retracting your use of my garden."

"But you two committed the greater infraction."

"We did not intentionally hurt someone," Psozela said. "Ours was the result of a research experiment. Our biggest infraction was not taking account for the possible effects of our experiment. Yours was a conscious and direct affront to the Cowav."

"I understand," Mrlfectori said. "I am still at the age where I am challenging life. Thank you for showing me this boundary."

Execution of Plan and Informing the Captain

Mrik had entertained himself with the Millium and the Plumerine Mystery for long enough. It was time for him to get the Zeposze together, gather all the information they had, and go to the captain. They would have to start preparing for their Jrath visit, and he wanted to make sure the captain knew what was happening in case they did not make it back from Jrath.

The Zeposze had grown used to their clandestine meetings and were ready when Mrik called.

Ssflora began the gathering by saying, "Thank you for entering the information I have been giving you into the Cowav. The information you entered into the FACTS level is starting to counter the Poloyal false information. You will need to continue, but we are also working on countering the Poloyal in the ANALYTIC level. The Scienctan are responsible for maintaining and upgrading the algorithms and formulas of the Cowav that are in the ANALYTIC level. I have confided in Sslonious, and as head Scienctan on the Empyramis, she has responsibility for the algorithms and formulas in the Empyramis Cowav."

Ssflora looked around and noticed everyone was attentive to her before continuing, "We have created formulas and entered them into the ANALYTIC level that will cull the information of level two for truth and eliminate questionable cells. It will take a long time, but with entries of information into the FACTS level and the culling of false information, we expect to have the ripple pretty much eliminated from the Empyramis Cowav by the time we get back to Arzola."

"That is great, Ssflora," Mrik said. "As we all continue, it is time I take this information to the captain."

Mrik arranged to meet with the captain in the privacy of the captain's suite. As the captain sat at his workspace, Mrik sat across from him and adjusted the seat as if he were going to be there for a while. He started telling of his meeting with Mrhonorix and finished with the plan to eliminate the Cowav ripple.

"This is of extreme concern," the captain said, "but it sounds like you have done an excellent job of handling it. We cannot communicate with Arzola without the possible Poloyal interception, and so we will continue with your operations. When we return, we will know how to handle the ripple of the Arzolan Cowav. I would like to have a celebration to show Arzola's appreciation to you and everyone who has worked with you, but I guess I will have to wait until we return to Arzola and get it all sorted out. Please tell all involved that I am truly appreciative."

Conversation with Mother

"Mom, the blending of blues with violet on your topper is impressive, and that little zirra really sets it off," Psozela said as she sat down with her mom at the Relux.

"It's hard to compete with you, but it is an expression of my confinement," Psril said.

"You have seemed sad lately," Psozela said.

"I don't like to think I have emotions you could detect."

"And yet the sun never shines with the same intensity in any two places."

"Perhaps I have been sitting under a shade tree too long."

"Could I sit under the shade tree with you?" Psozela asked. "We have sat under many trees together."

"I have always enjoyed sitting under trees with you, but I am wandering an unfamiliar path on life's adventure, with no definite direction. Perhaps that is what you can see in me as only you could see. My sadness, which you sense, is something I will learn from and live with until it passes on."

"I will always be interested in your thoughts and ready to sit under any tree with you."

"I have seen your sunshine wandering with Mrik."

"I've become quite close to him."

"I got to know him on Kovious," Psril said, "and I can understand his appeal, but you are getting close to uniting age, and you need to start looking at Politans."

"But there are no Politans like Mrik. He creates a feeling within me I have not experienced with any other."

"He is a Militan, and if you were to unite with him and become a Tradan, you would forsake one thousand two hundred and thirty-eight years of hereditary Politan blood you have in you."

"What is more important: happiness or hereditary line? Once I am in Pamatrical, I am just an observer, and while I am living, I want to be as happy as I can."

"But your two children would be Tradans, and you and they would not be in the great aura of the Politan preeminence."

"Would that be so bad?" Psozela asked. "Is living free from pursuing a legacy as a Politan necessarily a bad way of life? As a Tradan there are no airs of pretense. No pressures for perfection."

"But no feeling of being a part of the oldest hereditary line in all Arzola."

"What is the value of that hereditary line? If I unite with Mrik, our kids will have the genetics of both Politan and Militan."

"What about Proleb? He is a great guy and has been pursuing you since you were aware of men as different."

"I could live a united life with Proleb, but it would be like wearing last year's topper. Proleb is a great guy, and we could make an enjoyable family, but the zest, passion, and adventure are not there. Mrik is so strong and self-confident and acts like a Starmaster. He speaks with authority, and yet he is aware of my every aspiration. Proleb desires me for who I am, while Mrik desires me because he enjoys being with me. I have put Mrik into my Love Grid, and he fills all the spaces: feelings of companionship, respect, security, enjoyment, physical compatibility, group compatibility, mental compatibility, and emotional compatibility. No other male has even filled half of the grids."

"Your Love Grid has high expectations," Psril said, "and that is good, but sometimes high expectations are not in alignment with life. Uniting with Mrik is just something that you cannot do. I have spoken with the captain, and he is going to speak with Mrik, so he also understands uniting is something that is not acceptable."

"I understand, and I am planning on connecting with a Politan for uniting when I return to Arzola. But I enjoy talking and dreaming about the possibilities with Mrik."

Duludas

"Captain, an object is appearing on our view," Sslonious said. "An intersecting course. It appears to be a huge ship. It does not fit the configuration of a merchant ship or an adventure ship. I believe it to be a battleship."

"Stop here and set up our defenses," the captain said. "Put the bubble on max, and deploy the attack ship and the Trivacs to the back of the bubble. Open communication avenues."

"They have stopped outside of the bubble."

"This is Drux." A voice suddenly filled the command center. "I am supreme, and you need to submit."

"This is the captain of the Empyramis. We are from the Aolasel solar system and have no intention of conflict."

"Your choice is submitting or conflict."

"Captain, they have begun an attack. The bubble is diffusing and absorbing the energy, but I have never seen this much concentrated energy. I cannot predict sustainability," Sslonious said.

Then the attack stopped, and a voice could be heard again.

"I will come to your ship to speak with you, and I will return to my ship within four hours. Is this agreed?" Drux asked.

"Yes, agreed," the captain said.

"Mrbrixton, this seems like an unusual request," the captain said. "Work with the Cowav to develop a list of all the possible strategies Drux might be planning, and design defensive actions for each of them. I cannot believe that he is coming here for any other reason than to get information on our systems. He must have some equipment on his person, or possibly he will present himself as an artificial being. Either way, we need to protect our system from him. Let's plan a safe room in the landing area that will work as our reception area, which can be completely blocked from his intrusions. Then while he is attempting to hack our systems, we will be doing the same to his."

Mrbrixton, considering the captain's request, said, "As he enters our bubble, we can use the double-bubble system we developed for the Bogatars' attack, and we can run him through a sterilization process."

"Psimbrosia, I want you to do the negotiations with Drux," the captain said. "You will be in an artificial meeting room in the landing bay. You can be assured he will be trying to gain access to our information. Pay close attention to his attempts to infiltrate your mind, its waves, or circuits. If Drux is a bio form, try to learn his waves so you can access his memories. If he is not bio form, keep him talking as long as you can and on different subjects so we can analyze his circuitry."

"Captain, he is here," Psimbrosia said, "and he is digital. His legs are short, and arms are long with a large head. He is a little taller that we are, but his design indicates that the Duludas are bipedalintellect."

Drux said, "I am just here to make it easy on you. I have the weapons to destroy you, but your submittal would be preferable."

"But you have already tried and have been unable to destroy us," Psimbrosia said.

"I have just begun my attack, and I have any amount of time necessary."

"We have no schedule to complete. What is the purpose of your visit to our ship?"

"You could be of value to us if you become a part of our empire. Your destruction would not serve value to anyone. I would like to see the rest of your ship to see its value."

"That is not possible," Psimbrosia said.

"Captain, I have not experienced any waves coming from his command center, and I have not been able to connect with anything. He was talking when he came in, but now he is just looking around. I am experiencing a faint vibration on the floor. Maybe he is trying to use magnetic vibrations to hack our system? The way he is acting, it seems like this visitation might almost be a standard war procedure in this area, where each adversary surveys the other before they commit to a full attack. If this is the case, it would be important that we respond in kind. I would like to ask them for a four-hour trip to their ship. Drux cannot read Cowav communication, so he is not hearing our communication."

"It would be a very risky endeavor for you," the captain said.

"It is my choice, and I think it might make the difference in escaping this confinement. I will make the request to Drux. Have you found out anything on the vibrations?"

"We are experiencing the vibrations in an area around your location, but it is a technology that we are not familiar with and so do not know if Drux was able to hack our system. We have placed a magnivibra on maximum in the landing bay close to your location and a second one in front of the main Cowav center. Hopefully, that will disrupt any vibration hacking attempt."

"Drux," Psimbrosia said, "at the end of your four hours I will come to your ship for four hours."

"That is acceptable," Drux said.

"Captain, Drux seems concentrated on something—it must be the vibrations. He seems to be moving around as if to get better or different readings."

"At this point we can only hope their technology does not allow any hacking."

"Captain, I am on their ship now," Psimbrosia said. "They must not have mastered wave technology yet, because they are not interfering with our Cowav communication.

"I can pick up some very faint cerebral waves on the ship, but they are not strong enough for me to understand, and all the beings I have encountered are digital fabrications. These visits must be standard procedure, because they are not attending to me. However, they have prevented me from leaving the floor that I am on. It is an impressive ship, but I do not see any technologies that are beyond our knowledge except for the vibrations that I am also detecting here. They did have me walk over some plates. I think they were looking for vibrations. My four hours is up. I am coming back."

"Glad to have you back safe. Did they speak about their intentions?" the captain asked.

"Not at all. It was a strange encounter. I could not tell, but it almost seems like they are just playing a waiting game."

After two days of stalemate, Mrik, while in command of one of the Trivac ships, came up with an idea and contacted the captain.

"I can transfer to the attack ship," Mrik said. "It can make some waves, and I can ride them to the belly of the big ship, where I can plant some explosives. I would not have propulsion and would not be detected, but it would take a considerable amount of explosives, so I would take Arlam and Psozela with me."

"That sounds like a high-risk operation, Mrik, but we cannot deflate our bubble for offensive efforts without exposing us to their attack. I am not sure how long our bubble will withstand their attack. If you, Psozela, and Arlam are willing to take this risk, the whole ship will be grateful."

Mrik communicated with Arlam and Psozela about his attack idea and then said, "I hope you two do not mind me recruiting you for this mission, but you are the only two I know I can rely on for this type of priboarding."

Arlam responded, "Of course we don't, but I have never heard of using the priboard as a weapon."

"Neither have I, but it sure is coming in handy on this flight," Mrik said.

"What is your plan?" Psozela asked.

"There are some low waves coming toward us from the Duludas ships. We will have this ship create some waves we can ride to the Duludas ship, set some explosives, and ride the low waves back. We will exit through the double bubble. The explosives will be burdensome, but the concentrated waves from our ship will make for a relatively quick ride. Let's get our priboards and meet at the plank in ten."

At the plank, the three loaded up with the explosives and jumped.

#Nice, steady, even waves,# Arlam cerebral waved to Mrik and Psozela.

#The ship does not look very big from here, but it is growing in size rapidly,# Psozela said.

#There appear to be small ships going from the back of the main ship. Let's plan on setting up at that cove area with the green light at the bottom of the front,# Mrik said. #Hang on, here comes a Duludas fighter. He cannot see us, but he will likely disrupt the waves.#

#Arlam, are you okay?# Mrik communicated as Arlam was tumbled by the fighter turbulence.

#Arlam! Arlam! Where are you?# Mrik called out frantically.

#What happened to Arlam?# Psozela asked.

#I don't know. Keep going for the green light. Plant your bomb, and if I am not there in five minutes, head back for the Empyramis. You have to keep going. We must get as much of these explosives to the Duludas ship as possible. We will likely be destroyed if we cannot deliver a meaningful blow to the Duludas. I'm going to look for Arlam.#

#Arlam. Arlam,# Mrik cerebral waved.

#Mrik, I see you,# Arlam said. #Look toward the Mislu Wis galaxy, and you will see me. I am floating. I lost my priboard when that Duludas fighter swamped me.#

#I see you now, but these waves are slow. I am on my way. Getting to you was easy, but now we must get to the Duludas ship, with two loads of explosives and only one priboard. This will be some tricky surfing, but at least we have some good, stable waves.#

#I think you should leave me and get these explosives to the Duludas ship,# Arlam said.

#I would rather die out here myself than leave you, so we need to muster all our skills and figure how to ride these waves double with all this explosive. Here comes a good wave—hop on.#

The priboard caught the wave, but they were not able to develop stability quickly enough, and Arlam was thrown off the back.

#That did not go well. Quick, get back on. Let's try this coming wave. Just think of me as Ssflora. Hang on, I think we got this one. Good, now all we have to do is stay steady and let this wave take us to the Duludas ship.#

As Arlam and Mrik crested their wave for a smooth landing next to Psozela, they shared a quick smile, knowing their mission was still on course.

#Attach yours right here. These explosives are set up for the initial blast to propel the balance of the explosives further into the ship, so we have to make sure this flat side is next to the ship.#

They planted the explosives and caught the low waves back.

"Mrik, we have loaded everything on the Empyramis for quick exit," the captain said. "As soon as you are secure on board, trigger the explosion. We will use the waves from the explosion to aid our exit."

Massive explosion. The tail of the Duludas ship was still visible, but the ball of light came at them instantaneously with first red, then orange, then yellow light that surrounded them as they felt the Empyramis jumpstart their escape. The explosion probably did not disable the Duludas ship but would give them enough time to outrun any pursuit. Psozela, Mrik, and Arlam were still in a state of wonderment about what had just happened. Then, gaining a little clarity, they looked at each other and joined in a hug, expressing without speaking their knowledge that they had just saved the Empyramis.

Scot Simpson

CHAPTER 3
JRATH

Chapter #3 Jrath

Preparing for Stay on Jrath

The planetary room on the Empyramis has visualizations of the highlights of all previous planet visitations by Arzolans. It was the perfect place for the Zeposze to meet and organize their Jrath visit.

Mrik started by saying, "Around us we can see information on all the previous planet visitations and the difficulties they ran into. We can also see what they did that improved the lives of the natives. Let's start our Jrath visitation planning with the basics. Each group will have a livpyramis for living and safety. Psozela and I want to build a great pyramid for a galaxceiver and will need a tonxer, which we can share with Tsizmelia and Trelo, who want to build a gravomagnetic resonator."

"Those projects should keep you stationary for the duration of the visitation," Arlam said. "Ssflora and I will travel around Jrath and visit as many different native groups as possible."

"Rsoler, Hrlur, and I will also travel to different groups and be available to assist any of you as needed," Bruid said.

"Let's plan on getting together at far sun and near sun each year to discuss our findings, accomplishments, and to party," Hrlur said. "And before landing, place an orbiting transre so we can communicate. The Cowav should provide a list of all the other essentials for us to take for our two stationary and two traveling groups."

Visitation Landing

"It is time for Jrath," Ssflora said to Psozela. "I will no longer be anticipating your eccentric toppers at the Relux."

"I know, I am already thinking about what I can use on Jrath to make special toppers, and I will be happy to show you my tricks," Psozela responded.

"Thanks, but I expect on Jrath they will appreciate a little reality in toppers."

"I know, ladies, toppers are most important," Mrik said, "but it is time to make sure we have loaded all our supplies."

"As soon as the Empyramis lands we can unload, say our goodbyes, and be on our way," Arlam said.

The captain found Mrik and said, "You have proven yourself as a great Militan on this flight, and I cannot wait till we return to Arzola and you unite with a Militan lady and carry on the great Militan traditions. But remember, as the only Militan on your Jrath visitation, the rest of your group will be looking to you for guidance."

"I understand and will do my best to look out for all the Zeposze."

The landing was smooth, the unloading organized, and Empyramis was back on its way.

"Let's do our trans-global circumference and then stop for celebration before splitting up," Trelo said.

"The whitecapped blue waves flow into the multi-shades of green stretching ever higher to the light blue horizon, speckled with floating puffs of white," Ssflora observed as they started their tour around Jrath. "It is beautiful."

"While we are doing our circumvent, let's go over what we have learned about the Jrathlings from the preliminary Empyramis scanning and what we want to leave them with," Psozela said. "Their basic instincts control their lives. Knowledge of themselves is only what they have learned through their own observations. Communication is limited to their immediate group. We want to leave them with the knowledge they can create a better life and an understanding of how to do it. First, we must give them an awareness of their place in the universe and its celestial bodies and how they can use this awareness to assist their living. Then give them an appreciation of the importance of justice and equality, the basics of civilization. This will aid in their evolution to mutual living by showing the benefits of cooperating and working for a mutual cause."

"That is good guidance as we proceed," Trelo said. "Now let's celebrate before we split up."

"First, let's raise a glass of hlyusir to our conquest of the Cowav ripple," Mrik said.

"That was a challenge," Psozela said, "but now let's raise our glasses to the challenge of the unknown. May we venture into Jrath with strength and courage to live with, learn from, and teach the people of Jrath."

The Zeposze partied until their bodies told them it was time to get some sleep.

The sun was out and breakfast finished when Trelo said, "The gravomagnetic fields and celestial position readings I gathered on our trans-global circumference will get us pretty close to the best location for our gravomagnetic resonator. We are on our way. Bye to all." Trelo smiled as he and Tsizmelia set off in their livpyramis.

"We also have our general direction, so bye to all," Mrik said as he and Psozela boarded their livpyramis.

Returning his smile, Arlam and Ssflora headed for the long ,vertical land mass.

Hrlur, Bruid, and Rsoler also left, striding off to start on their random traveling explorations while waiting for assistance requests from any of the others.

Gravomagnetic Resonator

The spears were landing closer and closer. "Quick, let's retreat to the livpyramis—that one just missed my head," Trelo said.

"They are very accurate even at this distance," Tsizmelia said. "I could not gain access to their cerebral waves but am able to read the fear being created. We will need to get closer to develop a translation and be able to communicate."

In their circumference of Jrath they had developed a map of the gravomagnetic effects of Jrath and of the properties of all the celestial bodies affecting it. The place best for the location of the gravomagnetic resonator was right in the center of the Jrathan village, located on this large island just off the great land mass. Maybe they had an innate sense of the importance of the spot, but whatever their reason, it could not be as important as the gravomagnetic resonator, and Trelo and Tsizmelia could provide a better alternative for their village.

Tsizmelia was good with beings, so after a pause to let the Jrathlings stabilize their fears, she rode toward the village on her priboard and immediately grabbed the attention of the villagers.

A few spears came, but then they stopped. Some rushed to escape while others held their weapons and waited. After a long enough time for their adrenaline to slow down, Tsizmelia stepped off, watched, and waited.

The villagers were congregating and chattering. After what felt like the longest moment, one villager stepped forward and stopped, waiting for a reaction he did not receive. He took another step and then another. He was in no hurry, surely thinking this magical rider of the air would attack him at any time. He pondered each step with great trepidation.

Tsizmelia sat on the ground and put a string of brightly shinning goumia beads out in front of her. She knew this would attract his interest, because they all were wearing beads of one sort or another. The villager stepping forward was obviously the alpha leader, and it sounded to Tsizmelia like they were calling him Jrpo.

Jrpo continued his movement, and then he started to chat with Tsizmelia. Tsizmelia's Cowav was picking up his speaking and was also able to record some of the chattering of the rest of the villagers. The Cowav had no database of this language, but it was rapidly processing everything it was recording and was working on an interpretation. It would take a while and more input before the Cowav acquired enough language to give Tsizmelia the translation; however, it was quickly analyzing the vibrations from their words and giving her the ability to use her own voice to make similar words.

Jrpo froze when Tsizmelia repeated the last words he had just said. She knew Jrpo had to be running on adrenaline, and his last words were either threatening her with harm or gesturing to her with friendship. Either way, responding in kind was appropriate. Jrpo was confused and turned to his villagers, looking for their reactions.

They were just as perplexed as Jrpo and provided no response. Jrpo quickly turned back. He spoke a few more words, and Tsizmelia quickly repeated his words, still not knowing what she was saying. Jrpo was now about twenty feet from Tsizmelia and reassured by the spoken words without any indication of actions.

He continued his slow progression toward Tsizmelia. When he reached a spot about ten feet away, he sat down in the same position as Tsizmelia.

Tsizmelia relaxed. This was a sure sign a physical confrontation was not what Jrpo was wanting.

Just as Tsizmelia repeated his third set of sounds, the Cowav deciphered some of the words. There was not much to their communications, but Tsizmelia was able to give Jrpo a positive response, and she could see the immediate release of tension on the part of Jrpo and many of the villagers behind him.

Now Tsizmelia would have to begin the long process of integrating with their village and creating a plan for getting them to move.

Trelo had started his design of the gravomagnetic resonator. It would provide three functions. First, it would align with Jrath's sun and stars to give the Jrathlings information that would assist their living. Second, it would calibrate the magnetic forces of Jrath and the planets and stars that are affecting its surface. Third, it would provide the same celestial magnetic effects here for their baby's birth, as if she were on Arzola.

The small effect of the different celestial magnetic forces at the time of birth creates a surprising similarity in the personalities of those born on the same date with the same forces. Arzolan personal relations were sometimes understood by those intricate personality characteristics. When they returned, Trelo wanted their daughter to be able to fit in with life at home. So, it was important he create a similar celestial magnetic force on Jrath to what she would experience on Arzola on her birth.

The blue stones should provide the needed effect, and he could calibrate them to get the exact amount necessary to give her similar characteristics.

Trelo started with the blue stones. Creating the celestial magnetic effects for their baby's birth was timely, and they were not going to be able to delay that.

After about a month, with the help of the Jrathlings, Tsizmelia had designed and built a structure on a different location. She knew that to succeed she would have to make their new homes appealing. They had told her about their fights with the neighboring tribes. The Jrathlings made their houses with branches, so she designed a house of solid logs with a second floor. It took longer and was harder to build, but they could secure themselves and even throw spears from the second floor. They were impressed and started building their own.

The gravomagnetic resonator would be a gift to the Jrathlings. Built to last, it would give them a bridge to the greater knowledge of existence and an understanding of the intricate forces created by their planet and of the forces that were affecting it. But probably more relevant for them was the timing for the seasons so they could better coordinate their lives with their environment.

Trelo started the long process of explaining to Jrpo. "This gravomagnetic resonator gives you knowledge of the universe. It will let you read the stars and understand their relation to you. Images of the stars will help you understand them, like that group up there that looks like a bear with a long tail. We will organize them so you can tell the cycles of the seasons and when to plant your crops. One stone will light up on the day each year when the daylight starts decreasing instead of increasing. That point is the base of a calendar we will make for you, giving reference for all your planting and shelter needs."

Trelo knew they did not understand much of what he said. It would take a long time for them to have a good understanding, but the moving of the stones with the livpyramis captured their imagination and got them involved. By the time they finished, they should have a good grasp of the benefits of the gravomagnetic resonator and how to use it to improve their lives.

A few of the largest stones of the gravomagnetic resonator were too big for the livpyramis to move, and they would need the tonxer to transport them.

The birth of their baby was expected soon, so Trelo needed to get finished. He got everything organized so that Mrik could bring the tonxer and they could move the stones in a couple of days, then they would be ready for the birth.

The pyramid building was now well organized and could run under local control, so Psozela and Mrik both took the opportunity to deliver the tonxer and help with the final setting of the stones for the gravomagnetic resonator.

It was a half day's journey for Mrik and Psozela. They flew over a large amount of turquoise blue water then a vast section of land before coming to the great island. When they arrived, everyone was working, although Tsizmelia was carrying their baby, inhibiting her work. The coming baby's birth excited everyone, but right now their thoughts concentrated on finishing the gravomagnetic resonator.

Caral

The relub ball whirled past Ssflora's head, but her teammate was able to stop it. Arlam was on him quick, but he was able to pass it just before Arlam arrived. It was an intense game. Arlam made sure of that. He did not like losing, and although Ssflora could not battle him, her teammates—the pyramid team, made up of the pyramid workers—were better than his teammates, all irrigation workers. It did not matter who won, but it was fun and gave the Jrathlings a break from the laborious work of creating Caral. The Jrathlings called the game "relub" after the material they used to make the ball. Arlam designed the game to be similar to sisual, except when played it was on the ground instead of with poles in an orb.

When they decided on Caral, it looked like a good place. It is in the southern land mass, a dry area close to the ocean with a beautiful river that has ample area for irrigation and would make life easy. There also was a relatively large village nearby.

The pass was right on, and Ssflora's teammates scored. Ssflora could see the energy level in Arlam instantly rise. They had only lost two out of the last ten games, and Arlam always thought his team would win.

Just as Ssflora repositioned after the last goal, the ball was in play, and Arlam was jumping, swirling, passing, and headed toward their goal. Their long fingers on their feet like their hands gave them an advantage over the Jrathlings for jumping, and Arlam was taking advantage of it, even though there were no trees in the area to swing from. After his long drive, one of his teammates scored, and Arlam's banter began, just as typical as when he was playing sisual in Arzola.

"Ssflora, you need a relub topper to keep up," Arlam said.

Relub is bouncy and makes a good ball.

"Go ahead try another drive. I am on to you this time, and I don't need a topper to topple you," Ssflora said.

Of course, she liked to get in front of Arlam, because he did not want to slam her as he would in a sisual game, so she made him adjust.

Arlam's team won, but everyone enjoyed the game, and it was a good ending to their day of rest. Everyone went to bed energized for the next day's work.

Ssflora and Arlam had melded pretty well with the Jrathlings since they arrived, and the pyramid and irrigation projects were well underway. However, without a tonxer they could not build a large pyramid, so they decided they could get enough power and teach celestial information with a small pyramid. They were using the livpyramis to help with the lifting, and after they showed the Jrathlings the benefits of irrigation, they were eagerly working on an irrigation system.

It was early morning when there was a hysterical yelling, sounding like Caral was exploding. Ssflora quickly went outside the Jrathling hut Arlam and she were staying in, and there were spears flying and deadly fights everywhere.

"Arlam, we have to do something," Ssflora said.

"Yes, disengage your Cowav. I'm going to go get the livpyramis. That should scare them."

"But you can't do that. It is advanced technology interference, and not allowed."

"You are right, but I think this invasion is a greater injustice. Come with me so you do not get a spear through you."

Arlam and Ssflora scampered for the livpyramis. As spears started falling around them, they zigzagged, hoping to miss the directed spears. They made it to the livpyramis, where Arlam turned on every light it had, some with different colors and some flashing. Although the livpyramis usually flies quietly, he was able to create some horrifying noises that would have scared anyone.

"It is working. They are running, but how do we deal with our transgression?"

"The same way I dealt with all the sisual transgressions I committed in my career. Be happy they were not identified, and then forget them. The real intent behind the directive is not to use advanced technology to choose sides or to give them the knowledge to hurt each other. We did not choose sides or give them any information they can use, we did not hurt anyone, and we saved lives on both sides."

"I understand, but we cannot do this technological integration anymore. I have an idea to protect the Caralians without technological integration. Since we don't have a tonxer for a megalithic project with stone, we can do a megalithic project in the ground. There is a cliff by the ocean, and it faces the right direction for creating a directional constellation on the ground. It would not only teach the Caralians about the stars and give them north-south directional locations but would also create a mystical presence so great the neighboring tribes would be afraid to attack them. When we finish, we can leave them with other constellation diagrams for megalithic constellations on the ground to help them learn about the stars."

"That sounds good, but let's finish the irrigation project before we begin. I think the appearance of the livpyramis has sufficiently scared the neighboring tribe to give us time."

Building the Pyramid

"A beautiful bit of desert, next to a majestic river, with a large population, that best amplifies the gravomagnetic fields of Jrath," Mrik said, surveying their surroundings. "This shall be our spot."

"Not surprising—the locals also find this spot desirable," Psozela said.

"Let's land out of sight and make contact without the grand entry of our pyramid-shaped livpyramis."

They landed and walked close enough so some of the Jrathlings could see them and then stopped. They wanted to let them approach so they could hear them and the Cowav could learn their language. Their apparent leader slowly approached and said something. Mrik responded by repeating what he said.

Another Jrathling said something.

Mrik again repeated.

They were still a good distance away, so Psozela slowly walked closer and placed a gemstone necklace on a rock and backed off.

Their leader spoke with some of the others beside him then slowly walked up with his spear pointed at Psozela and picked up the necklace.

The leader looked at them and spoke. The Cowav was starting to put together a little translation and translated "good." Although he had spoken many words, when he heard "good," it pleased him.

The other Jrathlings spoke, and the Cowav picked up the word "peace."

Psozela quickly looked at him and repeated "peace."

Psozela was trying to connect with their cerebral waves, but she could see it was going to take some time. They were talking more freely now, and both Mrik and Psozela were feeding the Cowav their conversations. The translation was getting better when the lead waved with his hand, which obviously meant, "Follow me."

Mrik and Psozela paused. If things went badly, they could disable some of the Jrathlings by overwaving their cerebral waves, and they had their hand zasers. But they knew they could be overcome if they became surrounded by a large group. Psozela looked at Mrik and could tell he was thinking the same thing, but they needed to take the risk.

The Jrathlings were talking as they were walking, so Mrik and Psozela should have a fairly good translation base by the time they got to wherever they are going. They were also starting to coordinate with the Jrathlings' cerebral waves, and their thinking was basic.

They came to a small stone building and went inside.

The lead man said, "Two by coconut trees strange object dropped sky."

The man in the building whom they call Jrebizmiah asked, "What them?"

"Trying speak language," the lead man said.

Psozela said with her best translation, "Come far away sky. Peace."

"Why come?" Jrebizmiah asked.

"Things for you, and we learn your planet," Mrik said.

Jrebizmiah took a good look at them. It was obvious from the moment they walked in that they were not his neighbors, even though Psozela did not have one of her toppers on.

Then he said, "Go see Pharaoh."

It was a longer journey to the pharaoh's place, and his building was enormous. Giant columns everywhere were all are decorated with paintings, mostly of the pharaoh and a lot of writing in the form of small pictures.

Once inside, Jrebizmiah said, "Bow Pharaoh."

"Sorry, our custom not allow," Psozela said. "We peace cannot bow."

"Bow or enemies," Jrebizmiah said.

"We assistance you," Mrik said.

"Guards them confinement," Jrebizmiah said.

As the guards approached them, Mrik and Psozela quickly overwaved the cerebral waves in the guards' brains, and they were immobilized.

The pharaoh, whom they call Jrhufu, said, "What done guards?"

"They okay," Psozela said. "Temporarily disrupt thinking."

"What want?" Jrhufu asked.

"Learn planet assist your evolution," Mrik said.

"Don't know evolution," Jrhufu said. "What do us?"

"We show how build grand pyramids, teach about stars, weather, and seasons," Psozela said. "We help planet, leave, communicate us gone."

"Have plan?" Jrhufu asked.

"Sun planes pyramid seasons changing," Mrik said. "Reference for year."

They spent the rest of the afternoon and evening communicating as best they could, with the limited language, what they planned and how it would help them.

By the time they finished, Jrhufu said, "Jrebizmiah your contact. Help."

That was the break they were hoping for. Jrhufu had bought into their plan and was looking to help.

"Jrebizmiah meet morning coconut trees," Psozela said.

Sunrise came with the realization of the daunting task they had ahead of them. First, they must gain the acceptance of the Jrathlings, although some were already treating them like gods. They did not want the Jrathlings treating them like gods, but since all gods deal with the unknown, if they learned about the Jrathlings' gods, they should fit right in.

They had to explain the momentous tasks they all would be doing to inspire them so they would understand the benefits and knowledge they would gain.

Mrik started by giving the Jrathlings a summary of the project. He told them of making a great pyramid to reflex measurements and forces of Jrath and show the relationship to the sun. They would align the pyramid to teach celestial knowledge to help with their living and give an understanding of their existence. He also told them it would provide for the amplification of Jrath's energy and would be the location for the galaxceiver to provide communication with Mrik and Psozela once they were back on Arzola.

Psozela continued by telling them how they would help them understand and use the flooding of the Nolu River. She told them they would create a calendar based on the brightest star in the sky. This calendar would help them prepare for and understand the full year.

Mrik continued by unloading the tonxer from the top of the livpyramis. He started the long process of explaining how it worked and how they would learn to control it to move great stones. The other tool they had with them was the lectromag cutter, which Psozela showed them how to use.

When dusk came, the Jrathlings retired, and Mrik and Psozela began feeding additional information to the Cowav as it developed the building plan and schedule so they could finish in eight years.

The daunting task had begun. Their apprehensions and fears were put aside as they entered full force ahead.

Arlam and Ssflora

The rising sun awakened the horizon over the distant waves. The forested hills blanketed the opposite horizon as the sun sparkled from the ridges, and the tumbling waves broke on the yet-to-be-lit, lonely beaches.

"This will be the area of our next contact with the Jrathlings," Ssflora said. "I hated leaving Caral, but they are now totally self-reliant, so it was time for us to move on."

"Let's land next to that village," Arlam said to Ssflora as she maneuvered their livpyramis.

"They are just waking but coming up to the livpyramis and kneeling as in submission," Ssflora said.

"They must think we are superior beings, which I guess to them we are."

"Let's go out and assure them we mean no harm."

"The leader is speaking, and the Cowav is recording and figuring out a translation. I am not sure how to keep her talking, but right now that is not a problem."

"It appears they are asking us for help with their milit. It is their staple, and it is disappearing, and they are having irregular harvests."

"I hope they don't think we have anything to do with the missing milit."

"By the way they are acting, that does not seem to be their thinking."

"We should be able to help, but now it looks like they want us to come to their village."

"It's a celebration. I'm not sure what this drink is, but it must be intoxicating, because I would not consider it pleasureful."

"The question is, Can we make it back to the livpyramis?"

"Well, if we can't, at least we are among friends."

Two Days Later

"Ssflora, I think I have found a way to solve their missing milit. There is a middle-sized wild animal that will work well as a protector of the milit. They have a fierce growl and bark that would scare anyone away. They live in packs and are overpopulated. They should accept someone providing steady food. The Jrathlings call them dagles. I want to start working with them. Are you still working on their irregular harvest problem?"

"Yes, I went out and checked their fields, and it looks like they planted too late, and the crop did not reach maturity. We need to educate them about the celestial system so they will know when to plant."

"Do you have a plan?"

"I'm going to create a twenty-eight-sector lunar lodges star map they can use as a calendar to show them when to plant. I also noticed that they do not have any containers for storing their milit. Tomorrow I am going to do a little priboarding to see if I can find some clay and material for a spinning wheel so they can make pottery. Would you like to come along?"

"Sounds like fun, but I have my hands full with the dagles."

Arlam left the village and ventured out, looking for dagles. The first day he did not see any but had brought some overnight gear, thinking that this task might extend multiple days.

In the morning, he heard some barking and got on the trail right away. The pack had just made a kill and was busy and did not notice Arlam approach. He stayed a distance downwind, and on his priboard was not making any sound. He quickly noticed one of the dagles was skinnier than the rest, and the stronger dagles kept the skinny one from the food. She probably lived on the scraps that remained. She should be a good recruit for training to guard the milit. She would be appreciative of the food and probably not have a strong allegiance to the pack. Once nursed back to health, she would be strong and furious.

Arlam decided to wait until the pack was done eating to see if the shunned one went for the scraps. She did, and Arlam went in on his priboard with a net to throw over her. It worked, and he was able to corral her, but she was barking loudly, and the other dagles were soon after Arlam.

Ordinarily he could have just stayed out of their reach to stay safe, but with the added load of the dagle, his priboard was not able to go high enough. He did not want to drop her, but the pack was gaining.

He started swerving to evade their lunges, and then he saw a tree and quickly turned to it, lowered his priboard angle to increase his speed, and headed for the base of the tree. The pack was now nipping at his priboard. Fortunately, there was a branch near the base that he grabbed, and, with the skinny dagle tied on his back, swung up into the tree as the whole pack surrounded the tree. He was safe for the time being, but now he had to figure a way out of this predicament.

Spending the night in a tree with an angry dagle while the pack waited below was not the exciting hunt he had envisioned. He had two small knives with him, and he knew that rubbing them together made an irritating, high pitch. The sound was excruciating, but if it would work, he would bear it. It immediately got their attention, and after a few minutes, two of the five scampered away.

Naturally, the three left were the biggest and most ferocious, and they were responding to the noise with more aggressive attempts to climb the tree. After more time contemplating his predicament, he realized there were nuts on the tree. They were not big enough to hurt the dagles but maybe could create a diversion. He picked one and threw it as far as he could. The dagles heard it and began slowly inching toward the spot.

That is great, he thought, but not far enough to give him a lead to escape. As his mind raced for answers, he began thinking about getting the nuts farther away and realized there was a band around his net that was stretchy and would make a good sling.

He quickly crafted one and began slinging nuts at ever-increasing distances. The dagles followed the sounds of the nuts landing and reached a spot where Arlam felt safe attempting an escape. His dagle, whom he was now calling Dagip, was quiet, and so he tried not to upset her as he climbed down the tree and quietly boarded his priboard, staying low as he escaped.

A Week Later

"Ssflora," Arlam said. "Dagip is starting to bond with me and lets me know when there is danger."

"Is she accepting the Jrathlings?" Ssflora asked.

"Not yet, but they have indicated their understanding of the relationship and have started to take over. To make their relationship easier, I have developed some coordination with

Dagip's cerebral waves and have taught her to cover her own poop by scraping dirt with her back legs."

"Impressive. I have finished the constellation map and the spinning wheel, and it appears they understand. Their milit problem should resolve itself now, so let's say goodbye to the Chesue, as they call themselves, and head toward the setting sun for our next encounter."

"Snow-speckled mountains gradually flowing into peaceful valleys with structures that seem to be temporary," Arlam said. "This village appears to be nomadic. They are welcoming and showing no fear. They are looking for what we can offer to make their lives better."

"Let's leave them with some permanent and unique knowledge of this planet that will aid in their nomadic lifestyle," Ssflora said.

"The biggest decision they have to make is when and where to move to another location. We could make them a portable astrological machine. Let's call it the antiastrothra and align it with the stars. Once aligned, it will provide them with a calendar so they can know when the seasons are coming, wherever they are located."

"Tomorrow morning let's priboard into the mountains and look for some minerals that we can smelt to make metals for the antiastrothra. We can also show the Jrathlings how to smelt so they can make some strong new tools to improve their lives."

It was a beautiful morning for priboarding as Arlam and Ssflora headed out for the mountains. They spent most of their time just enjoying the beautiful countryside but found some minerals and burners and head back to the village.

"Tomorrow let's build a furnace to extract the minerals," Arlam said. "I'll add some rocks on top of the rocks on one of their fire pits and build it up so we can get enough heat to melt the mineral. While I am doing that, you can find some of the hardwood they use for their spears to make some molds for the antiastrothra parts."

The curious Jrathlings gathered around as Arlam and Ssflora did their tasks and showed the Jrathlings what they are doing. They picked it up quickly and joined in. With their help it did not take long to finish. They quickly saw the benefits of the smelted minerals. Learning the antiastrothra, however, would be more difficult.

It took a couple of days to mold all the antiastrothra parts and another day to put it together. Once Arlam and Ssflora finished it, they began instructing the Jrathlings on how it worked. Knowing that they would probably have to come back when the seasons changed to make sure the villagers knew how to use it, they packed up and headed for their next encounter.

They traveled over some beautiful country and were starting to enjoy the pleasant ride when a village started to appear.

"All those Jrathlings lying around with blankets in the middle of the day does not seem right," Arlam said. "Let's land. Now they are throwing spears and seem particularly hostile. I do not think it would be safe to try and help them."

"They must be frightened by the disease that is hurting or killing them," Ssflora said.

"They seem too aggressive for close contact. It is better if we leave them alone."

"I can assure them we mean no harm, and that should relieve their fears. I will leave the ship and try to make contact. You stay here in case things do not go well."

"I do not think you should go," Arlam said. "I will not be able to protect you if they decide to attack."

"There are many lives that look in danger, and we may be able to save them. There is no reason for concern. All I have to do is make them understand that we want to help them."

Ssflora was good at these situations, and if anyone could mellow these Jrathling, it would be her. Arlam did not think she should take this risk, but she had made her mind up, and it would have been almost impossible to change. She walked slowly, raised her hands, and turned to show she was without weapons.

She was not within spear's range of the Jrathlings yet, but they were already getting fidgety. She was moving slowly toward them, and although she was starting to receive some of their cerebral waves, they were not strong enough for the Cowav to translate.

The leader was in front with twenty to thirty around him, and some ritualistic dancing was going on in the background.

Ssflora wore a beautiful necklace, which she now took off and held out in her hand. They retracted a little, almost as if the necklace scared them, so Ssflora threw it behind her and continued to move forward slowly. She was getting into striking range of their spears.

They were holding their spears, but not in a threatening position. The Cowav was starting to translate a few words, and Arlam could hear her attempting to speak with the Jrathlings as she moved closer.

She made it up to where she was talking face to face with them, and Arlam was about ready to join her when he heard a big scream and saw spears going into Ssflora.

He was out the door with his zaser blasting in an instant, but by the time he got to her, all he could see was blood. There must have been twenty spear punctures, and some were still in her. He removed the spears and got her back to the livpyramis immediately, but her body was so cut apart she was already dead. There was nothing he could do.

All he could think was, *What just happened?* Ssflora's life, dreams of an exciting adventure and joyful uniting, gone forever. He just felt like going out and letting them do the same to him to put him out of his pain.

"Mrik, Ssflora is dead."

"Dead. . . . I'm not sure I want to hear any more."

"Nor do I want to tell any more."

"You need to come here right away. Do not do anything else; just bring her body here. I will collect the rest of the group."

It was what Arlam needed, a directive. He did not have to think or speak; all he had to do was follow the directive Mrik had given him. Mrik and Psozela were was less than a day away, so he arrived late that night. They were waiting, and stood and held each other for the longest time, feeling the common understanding and love for Ssflora. The next day Trelo and Tsizmelia arrived, followed by Bruid, Rsoler, and Hrlur.

Arzolans, with the help of the Cowav, control health on Arzola, and Arlam could not even remember a death other than during the end-of-life parties before life in Pamatrical. As a Militan, Mrik's training in death ceremonies away from Arzola reassured Arlam. They had an abbreviated Pamatrical party, which meant everyone could attend, and although the Jrathlings were not completely aware of what they were doing, they attended. The lummifying of Ssflora's body was particularly interesting to them.

They had to lummify her body by dehydrating it and then wrapping it in thin posiv ribbons of cloth so it would be preserved for the trip home. None of the spears had gone through her head, so once they returned to Arzola, her lummified body would go to the Pamatrical for reading and transfer of the imprints present in her brain. She could come alive again—at least, her digitalized mental being.

Arlam's Grief

"Arlam, I feel your special relation with Ssflora better than anyone, and you need to rely on me," Mrik said.

"We had been talking recently about the possibility of forsaking our heritage orders and uniting," Arlam said.

"I can't imagine the depth of your hurt."

"How are you and Psozela doing?"

"Ssflora was a precious one to us, and death is so strange. It is hard to process, but we carry on."

"Does Ssflora's loss affect your relationship with Psozela?"

"We have logically categorized the risks of our thoughts and feelings. It brings up our own pending decision. It is all about those fifty years of being united and raising a family. It would be mental anguish if I had to live those years without Psozela and continually think of how it could have been. When we were in Mysticwild, we worked as one. It was like our personal cerebellums were in total sync."

Mrik wanted to keep the conversation going for Arlam's sake and so continued, "I have never had a connection like that before, and it was the most comforting thing I have ever experienced. Then there is the feeling I get when we are in the middle of maximizing mysuvisx and I feel I am with the most amazing Arzolan in existence, and she feels the same way about me. I know I could find another lady who could make me proud, and I could enjoy being with and stay a Militan, but Psozela is my soul mate, and I am just lucky to have found her. Living with Psozela for the fifty united years would be like living in the sunshine compared with living in a cloudy day. So, I guess Ssflora's loss only makes me more aware of the decision I will have to make, with no good answer available."

After the Pamatrical party, the Zeposze gathered around a big fire they made and sat and stared at the flames, thinking about what had happened and how it would affect the remainder of their stay on Jrath. They spent the next day talking, thinking, and meditating, and the following morning they said their goodbyes—all except Arlam, who hung around with Mrik and Psozela for another week while he gathered strength to venture out on his own.

Hrlur's Fantasy Island

"How do you like that topper?" Hrlur asked as he greeted Psozela and Mrik. "The Rap Nu people like me, and although they did not replicate my face very well, they have done an excellent job with my topper. I keep telling them I am no better than they are, but I guess they like my topper, because they have created this beautiful, immense stone statue of me and my topper. I guess you can understand why I have it on now and wear it all the time."

It took Psozela and Mrik a full day to get to Hrlur's Fantasy Island. They described it that way because Hrlur seemed to delight in his position of advanced intelligence. His love for art, however, had directed his enthusiasm, so he had worked well with the Rap Nu.

Mrik was curious about Bruid and Rsoler and asked, "What have you two been doing while Hrlur was creating his artistic island?"

Rsoler responded, "We have been traveling around Jrath and exploring the areas all of you are not settling. Shortly after a visit with Ssflora and Arlam, we found a group of Jrathlings who were continually ravaged by neighboring tribes and just wanted to escape. They were good seafarers, so Bruid took flight to see if he could find a suitable place nearby for them to move. He found this beautiful little uninhabited island; however, it was a great distance away, so I created a constellation map and taught them how to navigate with the stars. Their whole village loaded up and set sail, and here they are now on Fantasy Island with a fantasy leader and his grandiose topper."

"They seem to be happy here," Mrik said.

"Yes, they are, and they have adapted well with the island."

Trelo and Tsizmelia arrived, followed by Arlam. Arlam was understandably late, as he was still in a state of disbelief.

Psozela wore a topper that she had recently made in memory of Ssflora and their topper rivalry.

Tsizmelia saw Psozela's topper, knew what she was thinking, and walked over to her.

"Greetings," Psozela said. "Did Tsillpill enjoy the journey?"

"Yes, she slept most of the way," Tsizmelia said.

"We brought some cine hlyusir from our village with us for the party tonight," Trelo said. "It is usually meant to liven up the party, but tonight it will provide just what we need to celebrate our remembrances of Ssflora."

"Arlam, you have come at just the right time," Hrlur said. "I have encouraged the Rap Nu people to extend their food supply by collecting the abundant manutar eggs on the neighboring island of Mot Nu.

"We use rafts to go to the island," he continued, "but they decided to make a contest of swimming to the island and retrieving the first egg of the year. The first one back will be rewarded with special privileges for the year. It is a long swim, and there are shrk in the water, and they can be deadly. I'm not suggesting you participate but just making you aware this competition is taking place tomorrow."

"Have you told Mrik about this contest?"

"No, I did not think he would be up for the swim."

"Mrik, Hrlur has just told me of a great contest the Rap Nu are having, and we arrived during this festival."

"Well, I hope you enjoy the competition, Arlam. I am just planning on a relaxing get-together."

"Apparently, this is just a little swim over to a neighboring island and a way to get to know the Rap Nu."

"What Arlam is not telling you is there are big fish they call 'shrk' in the water, and they are much bigger than we are and carnivorous," Hrlur said.

"Sounds like an event for you, Arlam," Mrik said.

"But it is swimming, and I should have no advantage over you," Arlam said.

"What about the big, carnivorous fish?"

"If they find me, it might be a good antidote for my thoughts right now, but if we just swim together, they will think we are bigger than we are and would not attack."

"So, you want me to swim with you so it is easier for the shrk to find us?" Mrik asked.

"That sounds like a good reason, and the weather is so beautiful here, a nice swim would be enjoyable."

"Enjoyable if you don't mind getting eaten by a shrk."

"To be a part of these celebrations and bond with the Rap Nu, I think we need to participate in this Manutar competition," Arlam said. "Here is my plan. We swim together and stay cerebral-wave connected. We each take a knife so if the shrk attacks one of us, the other one could stab the eyes of the shrk. If we do not see a shrk then when we get within one hundred feet of shore, the race is on."

"I will do this for you, but if I don't make it back, you must tell my parents and sister that I had a mighty fight with the ferocious, mystical sea god of Mot Nu."

The celebration was relaxing and partying great, and then the day of the Mot Nu race came.

"Over here! They are lining up," Arlam said.

There was a small cliff to dive off to get started. The water was clear and warm. Arlam and Mrik got ahead of the Rap Nu in swimming to the island, but Arlam had trouble finding an egg, so they were behind by the time they got back into the water. The waves were small, and the swimming was easy. They were trying to catch up with the rest of the swimmers and still cerebral-waving their thoughts as they swam.

#Arlam, I see a fin. It must be one of those shrks.#

#I'm coming toward you. Let's stay close,# Arlam cowaved.

#I can't see his fin, but he must be around here.#

#Maybe we can outswim him.#

#I don't think that is going to happen, since we cannot even catch up with the Rap Nu swimmers.#

"My leg!" Arlam screamed.

Bloody water erupted everywhere. Mrik could see the shrk behind Arlam and was able to pull his knife and go for his eye. The shrk was flopping wildly, as if he were trying to get Arlam underwater. Mrik's first stab missed his eye, and the shrk reacted but did not let go. Mrik didn't have to be concerned about the mouth, so he was able to quickly reposition and make a second attempt at the eye. Right on, and the shrk released Arlam and retreated. Arlam was flailing frantically with his arms to keep afloat as Mrik grabbed him, got him in a good hold, and started for shore. The Rap Nu on shore who are good swimmers quickly headed out to help.

"Am I going to live?" Arlam asked.

"I don't know, but before you die you will have a hell of a shrk story to tell."

Arlam was torn up badly. They were able to get him mended, although he would not be playing sisual anytime soon. At least he was able to enjoy the departing celebration. In fact, from his bed he was the center of the celebration and led the festivities. The Rap Nu were great people, but in the morning, the visitors were back on their livpyramis for their return journeys.

Taming the Animals

"Jrhufu is punishing his workers," Psozela said.

"Why would he do that?" Mrik asked.

"He says it is because they are working too slowly, but he knows we are on schedule. I believe he is anxious and just needs to show his authority."

"He would not receive our suggestions well. What could we do that would make life less stressful?"

"Perhaps a small animal could reduce his stress."

"Have you seen one that would work?"

"There is a small, four-legged animal with a tail, a cute face, and soft, cuddly hair that might work. I would like to spend some time studying them. Would you like to assist?"

"Sure."

Psozela and Mrik ventured out on their priboards to find wild cudruls.

"There is one over there," Psozela said. "He sees us. He is fast and is obviously afraid of us. I just need to get close enough to overwave his cerebral waves. He is hiding and thinks I do not know his location, but I am close enough to receive his waves. I read a lot of fear but cannot overwave his cerebral yet. Once he calms down, I may be able to have a minimal influence."

"He is too wild at this point to accept food from us. I think we are going to have to capture and hold him until we can give him an understanding of our intent," Mrik said.

"That is not going to be easy, but let's see if we can catch him."

Psozela saw him go into some nearby shrubs. She told Mrik to stay and approach slowly while she circled around back and tried to grab him.

Mrik positioned himself just far enough away not to startle the cudrul while Psozela ever so carefully approached him from the back. She was starting to feel confident and sprang for him. But the cudrul probably sensed her the whole way. It jumped as Psozela approached. Mrik was ready, but the cudrul surely knew of Mrik and went sideways. They scampered after him but lost sight.

Mrik picked up a faint cerebral wave, which appeared to be coming from near a small tree. As they got closer, Psozela could read some of his cerebral waves, but a lot of segregation was in his brain, making it hard to overwave. She could connect with some of his functions but not his consciousness, so they were back to trying a physical intervention. They located him behind a tree and came from either side to corral him.

"I got him. But not anymore, and now I have a nasty scratch on my arm," Mrik said.

"Let me see. Not good. I'm glad I brought my safety pack. Stick your arm out. What happened?" Psozela bit back a smile. "Could you not handle a little cudrul?"

"I thought you were going to pacify him with your cerebral waves."

"He has got a little of you in him," Psozela said. "He is going to do whatever he wants. I'm not sure how much I can curve his thinking."

"We can't give up now and let him think he has won. He went that way. Let's try using your sunfus as a net."

"My beautiful sunfus?"

"Unless you have a better idea."

"His waves are getting stronger as we approach the thicket. There appears to be a path from that thicket. I will circle around back of him, and you take the sunfus and stake out the trail. I will come up from behind and scare him toward you and my sunfus."

"I've got him, but he is still fighting. Shoot, he just ripped the sunfus and got out."

"You ruined my sunfus?"

"What kind of a sunfus is it that can't even hold a little cudrul?"

"A beautifully delicate sunfus that you ruined."

"This guy is pretty smart. What do we do now?"

"How smart can a wild cudrul be? We have to be able to come up with a way to capture him."

"Let's just follow him. We have to be able to outlast his little legs."

Mrik and Psozela knew that if they were going to catch him, they were just going to have to keep following him. After a while, the cudrul either got tired or thought that a tree might provide an escape, maybe not figuring that Holuas are good in trees. Mrik and Psozela cornered him at the top of the tree and grabbed him for transport back to the livpyramis.

"The way we coordinated our moves around the tree to catch the cudrul reminded me of Trelo and Tsizmelia's uniting," Psozela said. "I can remember imagining it being you and I."

"I had a similar thought, but just before I left the Empyramis my dad had a very direct talk with me reminding me of my obligations as a Militan."

"I had a similar conversation with my mother. It seems unfair, but it is the way it has been for centuries."

Once they were home, Psozela created a space for the cudrul, whom she was now calling Crik—most certainly because Crik's desire for independence reminded her of Mrik's similar feelings. Psozela created a space inside the livpyramis to give Crik a place to start adapting to a new way of life, but she also gave him an outside space as she gradually adjusted him to living with her and Mrik. After a couple of months Psozela felt good about Crik's progress.

"How is your cudrul doing?" Mrik asked.

"I think he understands I am not going to hurt him and will be of some benefit to him. He is taking his time but gradually coming around to me. He is beginning to enjoy sitting on my lap, which is comforting to both of us. His cerebral waves are radiating at an unusual sequence; however, I have been able to overwave his mind to influence his vocal cords. I am teaching him how to control his vocal cord vibrations so he will purr whenever the person's lap he is sitting on is relaxed. It will be a perfect way to teach Jrhufu to relax without him even knowing it. Let's see if Crik will sit on your lap and purr."

"Here, Crik, come to my nice, warm lap."

"It looks like he is not ready for you yet. He probably remembers your sunfus attack. His desire for easy food has overcome his fears of me, but I have not been able to teach him to follow any kind of verbal instructions."

"You must have had some luck integrating with his cerebral waves, because I can hear the purring he is making while sitting on your lap," Mrik said.

"It is very quieting and comforting. I've become so close to him I am thinking we should keep him and train others for Jrhufu and his family."

"It would be nice having him around, and maybe he will become comfortable with me."

"Wouldn't it be nice if we could talk to Crik?"

"That would be an interesting conversation," Mrik said.

"I don't think it would be possible with the small cudruls, because their vocal cords are so much smaller than ours. But I think we could make it work on those big cudruls that we saw the other day."

"Okay, while you are working with Crik, I will start working on a large cudrul. I'm going to contact Hrlur to find how to manipulate the cudruls' origin cells in their eggs to create a head like ours so we can talk with them. If Hrlur can provide that answer, then we'll just have to find a way to get a cudrul's egg."

Mrik contacted Hrlur, who, as a Healthan, had experience experimenting with life. Hrlur did not have any experience with cudruls but gave Mrik some direction and offered to instruct him on his origin-cell manipulator. Hrlur thought that if Mrik could get a cudrul's egg, he could manipulate the origin cells of a cudrul and the origin cells of a Holua to create a Holua head on a cudrul.

Now Mrik had the hard part of his task ahead of him: how to get a large cudrul's egg and manipulate it and then return it to the cudrul. He started by studying the cudruls, which took a while because they still were spending most of their time organizing the building of the pyramid.

It was not easy studying the cudruls, but he felt safe with his priboard. Although he could not outrun them on foot, he was faster on his priboard, and he could always outclimb them if trees were nearby.

While studying them, he was able to overwave part of their cerebral waves but was not able to gain complete control of their thinking. He quickly realized that if he had any hope of working with the female, he would have to take control of the pride, and that meant defeating the current alpha male. Then he could probably overwave a female enough to make her passive while he manipulated her egg.

The hard part was going to be taking control of the pride from the alpha male. He knew he would have to best the alpha cudrul himself but was thinking he would need Psozela as a backup.

"Psozela," Mrik said. "My plan to create a cudrul that can speak is ready for action. First I have to defeat the alpha cudrul, which I don't expect to be an easy task. So, I would like for you to be there in case things don't go right."

"I'm ready, but you know I cannot use any of our advanced weaponry on them."

"Yes, I do. I am hoping to connect with his cerebral waves, but in case I am not successful, I am taking this large gu ball for my head, which I hope will take care of his fangs. I plan to use a tree branch for his claws. I would like you to bring some extra gu balls and rope in case I need them."

Mrik and Psozela ventured out and found the pride of cudruls.

"I hope you are ready, because here he comes," Psozela said.

"His mind's circuits are very intense. I guess it's going to be a fight."

The cudrul lunged at Mrik, but Mrik lowered his head with a topper-like gu ball at the last second, and the cudrul got a mouth full of gu. But his claws got to Mrik before he could get his stick in place, and he was thrown to the ground.

The cudrul's fangs were incapacitated by the gu ball, but Mrik was struggling to block his claws after receiving the gash to his right leg. He moved to get on top of the cudrul and yelled to Psozela for another gu ball.

Psozela threw the gu ball toward Mrik, and he caught it just as the cudrul was throwing him off his back and proceeding to attack. Mrik swiftly moved the gu ball in front of him to catch the cudrul's claws. The cudrul retracted for a second to deal with the gu as Psozela read Mrik's waves and tossed him a rope. The cudrul was starting to work his teeth loose from the gu, so Mrik knew he had just seconds if he wanted to get this cudrul under control.

He grabbed the rope and lunged for the cudrul's rear legs. They were strong and still free, but with the mouth and front legs dealing with the gu, Mrik used his whole body to corral the rear legs—and just in time, as the cudrul realized what Mrik was doing. But it was too late for the cudrul. Mrik incapacitated him by encircling the real legs and pulling the rope, securing it to a tree. He still had a ferocious and angry cudrul with gu teeth and front claws that was not subdued yet but at least was stationary. Mrik used another rope to lasso the cudrul's head to completely control him for a good show as the females watched.

"Well, that is half the battle, now I have to pacify a female so I can manipulate her origin cells," Mrik said. "The females were watching with the rest of the pride, and I have their attention. This will take some time. I must get them to feel comfortable. I should be able to accomplish this by hanging out and overwaving with their cerebral to eliminate their fear."

"Let me tend to your leg while we let the tension in the pride calm down," Psozela said. "I think you have established yourself as the alpha, but you better see if we can overwave a female and manipulate an egg before the other males decide they want to contest your position."

"The female in the tall brush over there is the one that I have been most successful overwaving with, so let's work with her. I think her observation of my fight helped, because the overwaving seems to have reduced her aggression and made her receptive to contact."

Mrik and Psozela were able to manipulate the origin cells, release the alpha male, and get back to the livpyramis without any more problems.

"That encounter was extreme compared with our capture of Crik," Psozela said. "I can't wait to see the baby and teach her or him to speak."

Three Months Later

"I'm going out to check on the cudruls," Mrik said.

Upon returning with a delightful little kitty fluff, he said, "I think we should call him Zrphx."

"Wow, he is cute with our head and a cudrul body," Psozela said. "How did you manage getting him away from his mother?"

"It was not a problem. He was apart from the pride. He looks undernourished. I think they had rejected him. His cerebral waves are receptive at this young age, and I can overwave, though on a primal level. As he grows, our connection will also grow."

Two Years Later

"Mrik," Zrphx asked, "why am I the only one that has a head like you but four legs instead of two?"

"You are very special, a one of a kind. One day I will take you to see your mother, but now, whenever you sit out in front of the pyramid as you like to do, it gives the Jrathling a great sense of awe, which is good for all of us."

Galaxceiver Gold

It had been five years since Mrik and Psozela first started working on the foundation for the pyramid. It was a struggle and went slowly at first, but after they got the system down and coordinated their work with the Jrathlings' planting, harvesting, and building of an irrigation system, things were going smoothly. At this point their new reality seemed like home to them, and everyone was their friend. Zrphx and Crik made the livpyramis feel like a home. They still had a lot to build but were to the point where they needed to start constructing the galaxceiver.

The pyramid would collect and amplify power from the gravomagnetic forces of Jrath to supply power for the galaxceiver. It would sit in the center of the pyramid at the bottom of the tunnel they were building, directed toward Arzola. Once they left and returned home, they would be able to talk to the Jrathlings through the galaxceiver.

"Jrebizmiah, we need some of this pretty metal you have in your necklace to make our galaxceiver," Psozela said. "Can you tell me where we can find this material?"

"We call this gold. It is far away, and there is a different tribe controlling the land," Jrebizmiah said. "It takes fourteen days' journey up the Nolu River and then ten days on land to get there."

They needed to leave right away if they wanted to get the gold this year. They were thirty days away from the start of the flooding seasons, and considering that the flooding would start sooner upstream, it was important to get started. Twenty-four days up plus time to acquire the gold made for a long expedition.

Mrik and Psozela decided one of them needed to stay with the pyramid building, so Psozela took on the expedition for the gold.

Zrphx wanted to go on the journey. He was a good swimmer from playing in the Nolu River, so Psozela told him that he could go as long as he carried his share of the gold and supplies.

They were never able to develop direct communications with Crik, but she still felt like she was part of the Jrath family. Although she could feel the excitement of the journey, she would be more of a burden than an assistance and would have to stay with Mrik.

The amount of gold they needed could be carried by five Jrathlings, Psozela, and Zrphx, but Jrebizmiah informed her that they needed at least twenty Jrathlings to complete the journey.

They quickly set sail. With calm waters, a favorable wind, and the rowers, they made good progress, even though they were going upstream.

After ten days of smooth sailing, they arrived at rapids with large stones. They had to portage the boats around the rapids, which took two days.

After they finished with the river, it was a long ten-day hike to the gold village. Fortunately, Jrebizmiah knew the tribe, but before the group could get the gold, they had to accept the tribe's welcome and party.

Zrphx was the celebrity of the party, and he quickly mastered some basic words of the locals. Psozela learned some new dance moves, helped by their own form of hlyusir. It was a little wild, and she thought some of them learned some Arzolan dance moves, but she was not sure. By the time she got to know them well enough to be reciprocal with the dance teaching, she had drunk more of their local hlyusir than she probably should have. This tribe enjoyed life.

In the morning Jrebizmiah made arrangements for the gold, and the next morning they started back first thing.

The flooding had begun when they got back to the river, and they reached the rapids quickly. Psozela expected Jrebizmiah to land and start the portage, but apparently he was going to run the rapids. Maybe the water level was high enough above the rocks to let them pass. The water started to get rough. Psozela looked ahead and could see only splashing, swirling, eddies, and an occasional rock sticking up. Maybe Jrebizmiah had misjudged the water level. The gold was in her boat, but a lot of good that would do if they hit a rock.

Psozela wasn't sure what she was thinking, but she took a long rope and tied it around the gold and then around herself.

The Jrathling with the oars were working frantically, skirting the rocks, when suddenly right in front was a small rock sticking up just enough so as they went over it, it made a big gash in the bottom. Water started gushing through, and there was nothing Psozela could do but hang on as they took on more and more water. They were exiting the rapids but were going down quickly.

The other boat had made it through, but suddenly Psozela's boat was gone, and she was in the water, struggling to stay on top as the rope held her back.

Fortunately, there was enough rope that she was able to stay above the water, but she felt like she was in a waukay storm without her priboard. There was nothing she could do but try and stay above water.

She could faintly see the second boat, which looked like it had gone to shore. She was sure the current was too strong for them to row against. What could they do? Zrphx was in the front of the boat and was swept away quickly.

Psozela had tied the knot around herself tight, and being in the river with the knot wet, she wasn't sure she could untie it. Any attempt would be a last resort, because that would mean losing the gold. She was getting exhausted from her efforts to stay afloat when she saw something coming at her from upstream.

It was Jrebizmiah swimming toward her. She reached out and grabbed him, and they connected. Immediately she felt a tug as the rope tied around Jrebizmiah was being pulled to shore.

Luckily, the rope tied to the gold was long enough to reach shore, and they pulled the gold in. The Jrathlings were all good swimmers, and all of them on her boat, including Zrphx, made it to shore. But now they started the rest of the trip in a very crowded boat. At least the river was running fast, and oaring was not needed.

Psozela thought getting the gold would be the easy part of building the galaxceiver, but having braved the perils of the rising Nolu River, she was now thinking the construction would be easy. The galaxceiver would be transmitting all the way back to Arzola, so they had to make it precise. The specifications needed to be right, and they had to be careful the Jrathling did not inadvertently get exposed to the great electrical energy that would be created.

The Departure

Three years had passed since Psozela made her journey up the Nolu River to get the gold to build the galaxceiver. Things had gone smoothly, so Psozela felt great pride and pleasure when she said, "It is finished, this great pyramid, and the galaxceiver, and just in time. The Empyramis is scheduled to be back in one week. When we return to Arzola, all we need to do is set up a galaxceiver, and we can talk with the Jrathlings."

"Jrhufu is planning a grand completion ceremony tomorrow," Mrik said.

"I guess it is time for us to start packing."

At the Ceremony

"Jrhufu sure knows how to put on a ceremony, and his special hlyusir has me feeling loose and free," Psozela said.

"I have never seen this many people here before," Mrik said. "They must have come from long distances."

"I have really enjoyed life here on Jrath with you, Crik and Zrphx."

"I feel similarly. It has been the most enjoyable time in my life."

"It has been exciting, the environment is beautiful, the people love us, and time seems endless. Why would I want to go back to Arzola?" Psozela asked.

"It is a decision we have to make," Mrik said.

She sighed. "I guess it is tied to the question we have been considering, whether we want to spend our united lives together and forsake our heritages. This decision is like no other we have made or will have to make for our whole lives."

Mrik glanced aside then looked back at her. "When I think about the possibilities with you, I see the vastness but feel your closeness."

"We have been together as one through so many encounters," Psozela said, "starting with our naïve adventure to Mysticwild, then with the Bogatar, the hyper web, the Duludas, and most important, conquering the Cowav Ripple.

"I feel your strength," Psozela continued. "I see your truth and determination and am receptive of your vibrations and know my life would change as your consciousness grows."

"I would miss the Zeposze and my family," Mrik said, "but life is so well defined on Arzola most of the time, I am wandering through life as if on remote control."

"I understand. Feelings and life here on Jrath are anything but remote control. I cannot see myself going back to Arzola and looking for someone else to unite with, so we would unite and be together as Tradans. I cannot imagine you as a Tradan. However, you would look cute talking weather with some Albergsin trader over a cup of lula," she said, smiling.

"I always liked lula," Mrik said with a little grin. "If we stayed here on Jrath, we would not have the digital eternity of the Pamatrical. But who knows? We might live an extra hundred years to be three hundred years old."

Psozela touched his cheek. "We could have as many children as we want."

"We would die, and that would be the end."

"True enough." Psozela held his gaze, her eyes shining. "The best part would be living with you, knowing every day would be a new adventure. There are more things here to do than we could ever even understand. We could have a grand family, and we could make life better for many here on Jrath."

"I love the way you state it, but the Empyramis is landing, and it is time for another celebration."

This celebration was for a fond farewell. All the Zeposze had arrived, and the loading of equipment began. The members of the Empyramis got to walk on land and meet the Jrathlings.

Mrik greeted his dad, mom, and sister and gave them a quick tour of their work.

After the celebration, it was time to get ready to go.

Psozela found Mrik and said, "I do not want to leave."

Mrik smiled. "I was hoping you would say that. Let's go say goodbye to everyone."

It was morning as the Empyramis rose, blocking the morning sun as it lifted above the sparkling Nolu River, surrounded by green fields and palm trees. Crik was sitting on Zrphx's back next to Psozela and Mrik, holding hands at the base of the pyramid as they wondered what the future would bring.

Index

First letter of their name is the same as the first letter of their heritage order
*Second letter: **r** = male & **s** = female*
 # - indicates communication by cerebral waves outside of the Cowav.

Psimbrosia-------- Politan – Sixate
Sslonious --- ------ Scienctan – Sixate – Ssflora's mother
Tsillpill ------ ----- Tradan – Trelo and Tsizmelia's baby
Wiserdy ----------- Physically impaired, mentally advanced
Zrphx ------------- Holua head and lion body – lived with Mrik and Psozela

Heritage Sixate

Athlan --------- Asabatcy
Tradan --------- Trmur
Militan --------- Captain
Politan --------- Psimbrosia
Healthan ------- Hrapu
Scienctan ------ Sslonious

Years Prior To Present

1,457 – Arzola global government created
1,238 – Politan established
1,236 – Militan established
712 --- Digital life after living begins
576 --- Mutual life evolved
300 --- Cowav created
100 --- organized physical work starts

Life Cycle

3 years ------ baby
17 years ---- growing and learning
10 years ---- single – working
20 years ---- single
50 years ---- united and family
100 years -- single – legacy goal
200th year -- Pamatrical – life after living begins

Words

Arzola --- a planet

Biru --- a species on Arzola that flies
Catazumies --- a specialty food dish on Arzola
Cerebral waves --- waves that are created in minds as they think
Ciles --- a town on Arzola where the Clang live
Colink --- Arzolans' common interest connection
Cowav --- connection of all Arzolans' brain waves
Cudrul --- a wild cat
Lectromag --- stone cutter
Eluva --- a special event for male and female climax with mysuvisx
Empyramis --- the journey ship
Jiluma --- Jrath solar system
Fusa --- unique scent
Fuson --- a metal
Galaxceiver --- a receiver built for interstellar transmission of communication
Gravimags --- pyramids on bottom of priboards for using gravomagnetic energy
Gravomagnetic Resonator --- astrological instrument
Galwaves --- measure of distance
Halu --- exercising game in the Relux
Hlyusir --- a drink that loosens the mind
Holua --- the main species on Arzola
Kufina --- capital city of Arzola
Laximal --- national gathering area in Kufina
Livpyramis --- small pyramid ship for living
Lummifying --- preservative treatment by dehydrating and wrapping in thin posiv ribbons
Mislu Wis --- Arzola's galaxy
Mot Nu --- Birdman Island of Hrlur's Fantasy Island
Mysuvisx --- Male and female physical sexual engagement
Oluviam Hall --- Arzola gathering building in the Laximal Plaza in the Capital, Kufina
Originators --- Extraterrestrials that traveled and seeded planets with bipedalintellect beings

Overwaving --- placing one's waves over another being's brain waves to control them

Pamatrical --- location of all dead Arzolans' digital brains

Phi --- a favorite Arzolan game

Poloyal --- Politan group trying to take over the Cowav

Posiv --- special cloth wrap for wrapping bodies for preservation, similar to mummies

Priboard --- riding boards with gravimags on the bottom

Priyramelo --- apex room on the Empyramis – totally transparent for visibility

Rap Nu --- people of Hrlur's Fantasy Island

Relux --- area on Empyramis for socialization

Rollum --- a circular being, snake body two small legs and arms; wraps tail to head to roll

Sisual --- a traditional game in Arzola

Sixsup --- leadership group with one member from each heritage group; decision makers

Sunfus --- attractive scarf

Teratura -- one floor of the Empyramis devoted to gardens, nature, vegetation, and trees

Tonxer --- heavy load, pyramid-shaped transporter

Jrath --- planet in the Jiluma solar system and the Mislu Wis galaxy

Trextus --- a large and ferocious creature of Mysticwild

Trivac --- survivor ship that launches from the Empyramis during emergencies

Tuble --- mass transit

The Great Finunal War --- 3,000 years ago

Uncowav --- doing things outside the Cowav

Waukay storm --- wave storm

Xpys --- exercise area for the journeyers

Zasers --- weapons

Zeposze --- a group of Arzolans who grew up in Ciles

www.ingramcontent.com/pod-product-compliance
Lightning Source LLC
Chambersburg PA
CBHW050936120626
46552CB00001B/233